Kiss The Devil Goodbye

Kiss The Devil Goodbye

Lisa Marie Pellegrini

CHAPTER ONE

Tiger Lily, Pennsylvania was a clean and quiet suburban community. Its stone and brick houses and buildings were washed over in earth tones of tan and terra cotta. The only exceptions were the modern business complexes in the center of town, which were towering glass buildings with grey-tinted windows. They reminded Vienna of the buildings in the television show *Dallas*. Also in the center of town were some of the finer restaurants (like Stefano's, the quaint little Italian eatery owned by the mustachioed Stefano brothers Al and Sal), Tiger Lily High School, a smattering of shops and boutiques (like Delilah's, where Vienna's twin sister Juliet worked), and the hospital.

Twenty-year-olds Vienna and Juliet Mann lived on Clover Lane, and it seemed like almost all of their neighbors had some connection to the hospital. Dr. Thorne, a handsome thirty-something cardiologist who lived down the street from them with his wife and two sons, had his practice there. Dr. Thorne was one of those perpetually happy people. Sometimes the Mann girls ran into him during his morning jog. He always smiled, and when they asked him how he was, he always gave the same cheerful response:

"Never better!"

And then he bounded past them in his fluorescent green terrycloth headband and wristbands, his wavy blond hair bouncing up and down. "It doesn't cost a dime to be nice to people," he sometimes said. That was certainly true. Vienna thought he should start a second career in human relations books and books on how not to take life for granted.

For some reason, Vienna and Juliet hadn't seen him around the past few weeks.

And then there was Charlotte Sloane, one of Tiger Lily's friendliest residents and an inspiration to everyone around her. Charlotte was an eighty-year-old widow who volunteered four days a week at the hospital. On two of those days, she stuffed envelopes and typed letters, and on the other days she wheeled a book cart down the hospital halls and peeked into the patients' rooms to see whether anyone was in a reading mood. Charlotte was the perfect person for the job, always jovial and willing to lend a helping hand even before she was asked. On Christmas and Valentine's Day, she baked brownies or chocolate chip cookies for the doctors and nurses. She put individually wrapped hard candies, like butterscotches or sour balls, in the mailboxes of every household on Clover Lane. She remained anonymous, but everyone knew she'd done it. She was a tiny lady, not even five feet tall, but she had the biggest heart. Dr. Thorne's kids adored her. She was the kind of old lady everyone would love to have for a grandmother.

The Mann girls hadn't seen her around either the past few weeks.

Anyhow, the sad thing was that she *wasn't* a grandmother. She and her husband were never able to have kids. All she had left to keep her company was her orange tabby cat Butterscotch (named after Charlotte's favorite candy). Vienna's allergies prevented her from getting too close to Butterscotch. If she did, she'd sneeze uncontrollably. But Juliet was another story all together. She'd stroke Butterscotch's head and neck, and the cat always returned the affection by rubbing her body up against Juliet's legs. Then she'd scamper into Charlotte's garden and plop on the ground tiredly as though she'd just been chased down the street by a dog and needed a rest. Her amber eyes looked like two headlights as she flashed them at the cardinals and blue jays in the garden, watching them splash around in the grey and white marble bird bath.

Charlotte's garden was the most beautiful one in the neighborhood. Every spring Vienna looked forward to seeing the tulip bed in particular. Tulips in juicy citrus shades of lemony yellow and tangerine orange shared the spotlight with watermelon-red and bubble-gum-pink tulips. Clusters of fragrant lilacs hung over the white trellis that led to the garden, and along either side of the grey graveled walkway were lavender-blue irises and white and purple crocuses. The bird bath was in the center of the garden. Across from it was a white metal, Victorian style bench. Charlotte sat there on cool summer evenings with Butterscotch curled up on her lap, or on her days off with an open book in her hands (usually a celebrity biography or the latest murder mystery). The garden looked like a romantic hideaway, and Vienna was surprised that Juliet never paid much attention to it, considering that she was a die-hard romantic.

But those words didn't even begin to describe Juliet. The girl was obsessed with the very concept of love. She tore through five or six romance novels a week, usually during her lunch break at Delilah's Boutique or at night in her bedroom. She was addicted to night time soap operas, and she was always the first person in line to see the latest romantic comedy. She was an artist who used romance as the theme of her oil and watercolor paintings. Some of her paintings depicted a man and a woman holding hands on the beach under the moonlight. Several others showed a man and a woman in the throes of a passionate kiss or staring blissfully into each other's eyes. Four or five of her paintings were of a man and a woman slow dancing in a crowded, neon-lit nightclub.

And then there was the ever-popular heart motif, which Juliet incorporated into almost everything she wore. In the winter time, she wore sweaters and sweat shirts with red and pink hearts on them. In the summer time, she wore bathing suits covered with hearts. The wallpaper in her bedroom was white with pink hearts of all sizes scattered throughout. Her mirror was heart-shaped, and the frame was made of little pink and red stained glass hearts pressed together as though they were kissing. The pink lace, heart-shaped pillows on her bed were decorated with embroiderings of cuddling lovebirds and kissing doves. On her walls were heart-shaped plaques with beautifully scripted romantic quotes like "Love is forever." The glass paperweights and fancy perfume bottles on her dresser and in her curio cabinet were all heart-shaped. On her baby pink carpet was a hot pink, heart-shaped throw rug that she'd latch-hooked in high school. Her wristwatch had a heart-shaped face, and the stretch band was a row of puffed gold hearts. Most of her other jewelry and hair barrettes were heart-shaped, and she literally lived in her fourteen-karat gold heart locket. She even wore it in the shower and slept in it, and Vienna knew the reason why.

A photo of the man Juliet loved was nestled lovingly inside of that locket.

The Mann girls spotted him just as they were approaching Romy's place that morning. He and Cassandra, his daughter, were in their driveway opening the doors of his white Buick when he caught Juliet's eye. Her face lit up like Christmas lights decorating a mansion. She ran her hand over her waist-length, golden blond hair and smoothed her pink dress as she flashed her angelic blue eyes at him. She'd been dreaming about him for almost four years, ever since she and Vienna were high school seniors. Vienna knew it even though Juliet had never admitted it. She saw it in Juliet's flustered face whenever he came in sight. It reminded Vienna of spring time when flowers were just beginning to bloom, or autumn when the leaves were turning orange and red. Life began for Juliet Mann whenever he made an appearance.

His name was Maximilian Ward, better known as Maxi.

He flashed his teeth and dimples at Juliet, and he and Cassandra walked to the pavement to meet the twins. Vienna could tell that he liked Juliet from the way that he batted his dark eyes at her every now and again. Sometimes Juliet responded by smiling ever so subtly and puckering her lips a touch. Other times she batted her liquid blue eyes right back at him, and then she and Maxi would hold the seductive look for what felt like an hour. Time apparently stood still for them during those moments, when the rest of the world could all go to hell and all that mattered was the two of them, lost in a world known as Maximilian and Juliet.

Watching Maxi and Juliet make love to each other with their eyes turned Vienna's insides into an erupting volcano. She couldn't help thinking about what Maxi had done to her mother two years ago and what he'd done at her funeral three weeks ago. If only he'd stayed away like Vienna had asked him to do.

"Hi, Juliet."

"Hello, Maxi."

This was the first time their eyes were meeting since the funeral. Vienna knew that if it hadn't been for the scene she caused, Maxi and Juliet would be together now, which didn't make any sense to Vienna.

Maxi was forty and Juliet was almost twenty-one. What could they possibly have in common?

Cassandra was looking perky and cheerful in her smiley-face T-shirt and white slacks, and her dark hair looked cute pulled back in a pony tail. "Vienna, are we still on for tonight?" she asked in her chipper voice.

Vienna was planning to spend the night at her house. They were going to watch a marathon of Julia Roberts movies on one of the cable channels.

"Sure, Cass. I'll be there as soon as my class is over."

Vienna was on her summer break from Columbia University, and she was taking a couple of night classes at Tiger Lily High, hoping to brush up on her computer and business skills. She was also looking for a summer office job, although she worried a little about what her chances would be at finding one. It was already the middle of May, and many college students had summer jobs lined up before the end of the school year.

"Say, what's up with all our neighbors?" Vienna asked. "Jules and I haven't seen anyone around in weeks."

Cassandra nodded. "I haven't either."

Even the animals seemed to be in hiding, except for the two robins and three sparrows that were chirping joyfully as they hopped across the gravel in Charlotte's garden.

"It's like something bad is about to happen, and they're all staying inside and locking their doors for fear of whatever it is," Vienna said.

Maxi smiled. "Typical Vienna. Always dark and brooding."

Vienna shot a cold look at him.

"I don't really care why this street's been so dead," Cassandra said. "I'm just thrilled that tomorrow is Friday. Feels like it takes forever to get here."

"Hang in there," Vienna said. "Only one more month before you graduate."

"You're not going to the boutique yet, are you?" Maxi asked Juliet. He glanced at his watch. "It's only seven-fifteen."

"We're stopping off at Romy's first, then I have a few errands to run before work. Vienna has an interview at ten-thirty."

He nodded, not bothering to wish Vienna good luck, but she didn't feel slighted. She despised him too much to care.

"Dad and I are heading off to school now," Cassandra said.

Maxi had been teaching English at Tiger Lily High for seventeen years, but he'd never taught Vienna and Juliet. Vienna was thrilled about that, but she knew Juliet wasn't.

"Cass, you're so lucky," Juliet said. "You have your own personal chauffeur. You don't have to wait for the bus."

A warm breeze gently ruffled the red and white flowers of the dogwood trees and azalea bushes that lined the brick and stone houses of Clover Lane. Spring time weather was perfect in Tiger Lily. The sun was always shining brightly, and the temperature remained in the seventies, so no one ever had to wear anything heavier than a windbreaker, even in the evenings. Another breeze came along and shuffled the red and white petals on the pavement, making them skip and dance so quickly that they looked like a whirling blur of little candy canes. Juliet smiled softly as the breeze blew Maxi's dark hair out of place. Apparently she liked him with mussed up hair. Seeing him all dressed up in his light grey, double-breasted suit also got her heart jumping. Vienna could tell because Juliet wouldn't take her eyes off him. You would have thought that *People Magazine's* Sexiest Man Alive had just set foot on Tiger Lily terrain.

Juliet stepped a little closer to him, maybe because she liked the musky scent of his cologne. With those few steps, she almost lost her balance because of the uneven pavement below. Maxi took hold of her arm to keep her from tripping.

"Careful, Jule."

Vienna supposed that he enjoyed being Juliet's own personal Superman, the man who made sure that he and no one else would always be around to rescue the beautiful damsel in distress. That was why he'd flown to her side at the funeral three weeks ago, but Vienna didn't want to think about that.

"Thank you, Maxi," Juliet said.

"So how have you been?" he asked a little awkwardly, as though he felt ashamed for not calling her over the past few weeks. "How's work at Delilah's?"

"Great. We've been very busy because of the half-price sale."

"I've been meaning to stop by and say hi," he said. "Are you applying to art schools now?"

"No, I'm putting that off for another year or two while I save a little more money. I'm working on some new paintings though."

"Will you show them to me some time?" he asked.

"Only if you let me take that Shakespeare class you're teaching in June."

"Sorry, Juliet, I can't."

"Then I guess you'll never see my drawings," she said with a playful gleam in her eyes.

"Now, I'm sure I can find some way to persuade you."

"Well, when you think of something, let me know, Maxi."

He peered at her with amusement in his eyes—and a flicker of intimacy, too. Juliet returned the look with a wink and a smile. Vienna and Cassandra exchanged a look of uneasiness. Vienna was appalled that Juliet was flirting with her friend's father right in front of her friend.

"Jules, we better get going," Vienna said impatiently.

"I like that scent you're wearing, Jule," Maxi said. "What is it?"

"Rose-scented body lotion."

Juliet and Maxi gazed at each other as though chubby little Cupid had put a spell on them.

"I like it, too, Jule," Cassandra chimed, interrupting their moment. Vienna was glad. "Can I borrow it some time?"

"Sure, Cass. I'm sorry, we have to go." Juliet gave Maxi one last smile, a big and beautiful one. "Goodbye, Maxi." Vienna grimaced. Juliet may have been saying goodbye verbally, but the tone of her sweet, girlish voice seemed to be saying, "Call me some time."

Vienna and Juliet continued on their way to Romy's. Maxi and Cassandra walked back up their driveway to the car. Vienna caught Juliet turning her head and giving him one last look.

At that very same moment, he looked up from his car and peered at Juliet.

CHAPTER TWO

"Jules, I can't believe you were flirting with him right in front of Cassandra."

"I wasn't flirting."

"Okay, girls, let's not start," Romy said.

Romaine Confidelle lived four houses down the street from them, next door to Charlotte. She took care of Butterscotch whenever Charlotte went away for a week or two to visit her niece in Arizona. While she was away, Juliet loved to go to Romy's and play with Butterscotch.

Romy and Felicity (the twins' mother) had been best friends for twenty-three years, since their sophomore year at Tiger Lily High. They worked in the human resources department of Pinkerton, Inc., an investment company in one of those towering modern business complexes in the center of town. They'd eaten lunch together every day, traveled together, and shared a sisterly bond, knowing each other's flaws and idiosyncrasies in the same way that Vienna and Juliet understood each other. Romy was like the aunt that the Mann girls never had.

"Romy, we need to talk to you about our mom's suicide," Vienna said.

The police had found Felicity's body three weeks ago, on an unusually chilly day in late April. Her black Honda Accord, speckled with frost that glittered like diamonds, was parked on the side of a grey highway that saw no life of any kind. Not even the greenery of grass or a bush, or even a leafless tree whose spindly branches had yearned for days gone by. Felicity's body was slumped over the blood-soaked steering wheel. The silver .38 revolver lay on the dusty black car mat near her right foot, stained by droplets of blood that had dripped from the steering wheel. The crimson-splotched suicide note on the dashboard of the car read:

"He hurt me! He violated my trust and he hurt me. I feel so ashamed, so guilty. What would people say behind my back if they knew? It's over, all of it."

Felicity couldn't love anyone else after her husband died. Vienna and Jules never knew their father. He died in a household fire when Felicity was eight months pregnant with them. Her loss had been so severe that she couldn't even bring herself to look at his photos without crying. She tore them up and threw them away, so unfortunately, the girls never even saw what he looked like. They asked Felicity to take them to his grave, but she'd had him cremated. She told them that she'd sprinkled his ashes over the park near their house. That was where she and her husband had met when she was sixteen and he was a twenty-three-year-old legal clerk. They hit it off instantly after she told him she was planning to major in political science or pre-law in college. Love bloomed rapidly, and the two were married a year later, but she deferred her college plans after she became pregnant at eighteen.

The Mann girls wondered how their father would have liked having twin daughters. He probably would have wanted to try again for a son and wouldn't have liked being outnumbered in a house full of women. The girls laughed about that sometimes. It gave them some amusement, in light of the fact that they never knew him.

"I think you should take a look at this, Romy," Vienna continued.

She took the letter out of her black leather purse and handed it to Romy, who read it in silence and then folded it in half and put it on the mahogany coffee table. Romy looked at it for a while as she sat on the sofa with her hands resting on her crossed legs, as though she didn't know what to make of it. Vienna leaned forward in the beige leather recliner, waiting impatiently for a reaction of some sort—a gasp, a cry of disbelief. Something.

But Romy uttered no response of any kind. Her eyes rested on a crystal-framed photo of Felicity and herself that was propped on the mantel. Best friends on their way to the senior prom, all dressed up in satin and smiles. Felicity's red hair shone like copper against her black, off-the-shoulder gown. Beside that photo was a photo of Felicity and the twins at their high school graduation. Felicity was standing proudly in between Juliet and Vienna with one arm around each of them as they posed in those sweltering robes.

The silence infuriated Vienna so much that she wanted to scream. Romy continued to sit pensively, her head tilted to one side in a melancholy fashion and her brown hair falling over her white blouse. Her brown eyes filled with tears. She blinked, and the tears spilled down her pink-rouged cheeks. Her eyes moved listlessly down to the black and tan Oriental carpet beneath the coffee table. Between her index finger and thumb, she rubbed the fourteen-karat gold filigree cross around her neck, the one she'd bought in Florence during her two-week trip to Italy with Felicity two years ago. Romy was a good Catholic who attended mass every Sunday. Her eyes swept over the wooden crucifix on the wall and the porcelain statue of the Blessed Mother on the mantel. Romy was obviously relying on her faith to help her deal with this tragedy.

In the meantime, Vienna turned her attention to the aquarium atop Romy's bay window, hoping the red and blue Siamese fighting fish swirling around in there would relax her and take her mind off of the irritating silence. She studied the beautiful bonsai tree on the coffee table and mentally escaped for a few minutes in the lush and leafy forest green branches.

"What do you think, Romy?" she asked, unable to stand the quiet any longer.

Romy looked up at the girls as she wiped the tears from her cheeks. "I have no idea. The letter is too brief. It doesn't give us much to go on."

"We think she was raped."

"*You* think so," Juliet said.

"Right, and I think Maxi is our man," Vienna added.

"No, he wouldn't rape anyone," Romy said.

"He used to hit her!"

"That was two years ago," Juliet said. "He's not like that anymore. Not since he went into therapy."

"I think he should *still* be in therapy," Vienna said.

"He was getting along fine with Mom before she died. She forgave him a long time ago."

"Romy, do you have any idea who this man is?" Vienna asked. "A friend? A boyfriend we didn't know about?"

"No, she didn't have any male friends."

"It's got to be Maxi," Vienna muttered. "Damn him!"

Juliet's cherubic blue eyes turned hard and menacing, and she pouted her lower lip in disdain. Vienna could see that Juliet was getting ready to pounce on her just like Butterscotch liked to pounce on yarn whenever Charlotte sat in the garden and knitted something. God forbid anyone speak an unkind word about Maxi in Juliet's presence. In her mind, wicked souls could be magically redeemed into respectable and harmless citizens. Some people considered that outlook positive and open-minded. Vienna thought it was foolish and naïve.

"Maxi didn't do anything," Juliet said. "He's a wonderful man."

Vienna eyed her suspiciously. "Are you screwing that bastard?"

"I'm not sleeping with him, no."

"I asked him not to come to Mom's funeral," Vienna said. "Not only did he disrespect my wishes and show up, but he was all over you, too!"

"He was just consoling me, Vien."

"It looked like a lot more than consolation, Jules."

"You didn't have to punch him out right there at the cemetery!"

"Look, Jules, I know you see Maxi as a father figure, and I know he was very kind and compassionate to you after your break-up with Richard, but still—"

"Please, don't bring *that* up. You shouldn't have punched Kelly Kline and Richard either—and right on the football field in front of half the school!"

"Well, I knew that jerk was cheating on you with her," Vienna said. "If we could live our senior year in high school all over again, I'd do the same damn thing. I hate seeing people walk all over you."

"Richard and I had an understanding. We weren't exclusive. I didn't love him."

"No, you love Maxi," Vienna said. "And that scares me even more."

"I'm not involved with him. I've never even kissed him!"

Juliet said that with a touch of longing in her voice, then she lowered her eyes and said nothing more. Her lower lip quaked a little, as though she wanted to cry, so Vienna left her alone. It broke her heart to see Juliet look that way.

"I'm sorry, Jules. You know I'm just trying to look out for you."

"Vienna," Romy said, "Maxi hit your mom because he was going through a rough patch after his wife died, and he was angry at the world. Unfortunately, he took his anger out on Felicity.

But it's been five years since she died, and he's accepted it. It's obvious from his demeanor. If you think about the way he acted back then and his behavior now, it's like night and day. He's a good man. I've known him for over twenty years, since your mom and I went to high school with him. He's had a lot of obstacles to overcome in his life, and he hasn't always dealt with them in the best way, but he's a fighter and a survivor. I think he's proven that. He's back on track again. He and Cassandra are doing just fine."

"What was he like as a teenager, Romy?" Juliet asked. The weepy look on her face had vanished. She was smiling brightly now, like a rainy day that suddenly turned clear and sunny.

"He was a little shy, believe it or not."

Vienna laughed. "Maxi Ward? Shy?"

"In a way. Not that he wasn't mischievous at times, because he was. But he was bashful in class. He sat in the back of the room, in the last row. He didn't like to raise his hand or participate very much in the discussion. And if the teacher called on him, his face got red."

"I can see that about him," Juliet said. "Maybe that's why he won't let me take his Shakespeare class. He's self-conscious, and he's afraid I won't like his teaching technique."

Romy leaned forward on the sofa, her hands folded together calmly. "Listen, girls, this hasn't been an easy time for any of us. Your mom was like a sister to me. Everyone at Pinkerton misses her, too. But the only thing we can do is try to get back into the swing of things and resume a normal life. I have no idea who this man is that she's referring to in her note, and I don't see how we can ever find out. There comes a time in life when you have to realize that some problems just can't be solved. Unfortunately this is one of them. Please, let it go."

CHAPTER THREE

"Excuse me, do you have this bag in pink?"

A striking blond, thirty-something woman with violet-blue Elizabeth Taylor eyes was browsing at the evening bags on the wooden shelves against the wall in Delilah's Boutique. Juliet had just received a shipment of them in an assortment of pastel colors. The one the blond was asking about was an envelope style, white satin purse.

"We don't have any right now," Juliet said. "We have a couple of other pink bags in a scallop shape." She pointed to the sequined bags on the shelf below.

The woman twitched her mouth in a show of dissatisfaction. "I like the other style better."

Juliet nodded. "We'll be getting another shipment next week. If you'd like, I can put one aside for you when they come in."

"Oh, that would be great. I've been looking for something like this to bring to a few weddings in June, but I can't seem to find one I like in pink."

"It's a popular color for spring. It sells fast." Juliet smiled. "I'll be happy to take down your name and number and let you know when they come in."

"I'd appreciate that. My name is Miranda Key."

Juliet jotted that down on a small, spiral-ring note pad along with Miranda's phone number.

Miranda smiled. "Thanks a lot."

"No problem! If you need help with anything else, just let me know."

Miranda glanced at the shimmering evening gowns as she headed toward the door, apparently drawn to the lovely shades of aqua, mint green, and periwinkle. Juliet liked her fashion sense and admired how well she color-coordinated her clothes and accessories. Miranda was wearing a pale yellow blazer with a matching skirt and pale yellow, high-heeled ankle strap shoes. Under her arm she was carrying a subdued yellow, patent leather clutch purse. A sparkling, pear-shaped yellow gemstone, suspended from a gold snake chain, adorned her neck. Dangling from her earlobes were matching earrings. Juliet didn't know what the stone was. Citrine? Yellow sapphire? Canary diamond? Whatever it was, this woman had style.

The silver bell above the door tinkled happily as Miranda left. Ten minutes later, the bell jingled again. Juliet looked up to see Maxi. He was so handsome in his light grey suit, grey shirt, and matching silk tie. She smiled softly as she thought about how he'd saved her from tripping on the sidewalk that morning. He was such a gentleman.

"Hello, Maxi," she said as she came out from behind the glass counter that displayed the leather wallets and other accessories. "Did you change your mind about the Shakespeare class?"

"Sorry, but no. I just wanted to say hi."

She checked her watch. It was six o'clock. "It's actually closing time."

He chuckled. "So now you're going to throw me out? You really want to get in that class, don't you?"

"I'm not throwing you out," she said as she headed toward the door to flip over the black and white 'Open' sign in the window.

"I like your dress," he said. "Baby pink is a good color on you."

"Thanks, Maxi."

The Righteous Brothers' soft, melodious "Ebb Tide" began to play on the little portable radio behind the cash register.

"I love this song!" she cried. She scooted up to the register and turned up the volume, then she dashed back to Maxi and took him in her arms. "Let's dance."

"I'm not very good, Jule."

"I doubt that. Besides, this is my favorite song, and you're the only man in the room."

He laughed softly as they glided across the floor in each other's arms. Maxi's laugh was always tranquil and soothing to her ears. She wondered whether her father had a laugh like that, or whether he and Felicity had ever danced for the hell of it, like she and Maxi were doing right now. Sometimes Juliet liked to think about little, insignificant things like that just because it made her feel connected to her father's spirit in some small way. She wished that she could dance with her father at her wedding some day. Who was going to give her away? Vienna? Romy? Maxi certainly couldn't. He was the man Juliet wanted to marry. She wondered whether her father had been anything like him, or whether he looked at all like him.

"What's so funny, Maxi?"

"Every time I hear this song, I think about the time I was working as a waiter at this cozy little Italian restaurant in my junior year at Villanova. One night I was carrying two trays of pasta down a flight of stairs, and I slipped and fell. The food went flying. Dishes crashed all over the floor. I had sauce stains on my clothes. I even had sauce in my hair, along with a few pieces of corkscrew pasta."

Juliet laughed. "I wish I could have seen you."

"My boss' face looked almost as red as the sauce. He was just about to let me have it when a very dapper, distinguished old gentleman in an Italian silk suit stood up and said, 'Don't you fire that kid! I'll pay for every one of those meals.'"

"A guy with a heart," she said.

"He was a regular customer of mine. He came in every Thursday night dressed to the nines, and he always sat in the corner booth, below a black and white photo of Frank Sinatra—his favorite singer. And he always ordered the most expensive thing on the menu—lobster tail. That man gave me my best tips. Anyway, 'Ebb Tide' was the song that was playing on the night of that pasta catastrophe." He started to laugh again, flashing a gorgeous set of teeth and those adorable dimples that made her smile. "That was also the night this lady in a black veil lit a cigarette, and the veil caught fire, so the busboy dumped a pitcher of water on her head. Oh, I could tell you all kinds of stories. The owner had a lady friend who used to come in with her toy poodle. She used to sit him in a high chair, put a bib around his neck, and cut up filet mignon for him. Prime rib, lamb chops, king crab legs—you name it. That dog had the life."

"Maxi, you're making this up!"

"No, I'm not. I'll take you there some day. You can ask the owner. He's up in years now, but he loves the place and doesn't want to sell it. And I visit every now and then. I've got some great memories from that time of my life. You would have loved the owner's white Persian cat Bianca. Sometimes he brought Bianca to the restaurant, and he cut up a grilled tuna steak and fed it to her." He smiled. "When I was a kid, my mom used to talk to our cat in Italian. She'd ask him if he wanted tuna, and he'd follow her into the kitchen."

"Your mom was Italian?"

He nodded. "She was born in Rome. Her family came here when she was five."

Juliet smiled. "I never knew you were half Italian. I am, too. My dad was Italian. Remember that trip to Italy I took with my mom and Vienna three years ago? We saw stray cats crawling all over Venice. Crossing the bridges, strolling through St. Mark's Square—everywhere. Vienna's allergies acted up like crazy. She had a sneezing fit like you wouldn't believe, and she broke out into so many rashes that she was ashamed to leave the hotel."

"You did some great sketches of the Coliseum. Maybe some day you can draw *me*."

"I'd love to, Maxi."

She thought about her conversation with Vienna that morning, when she said that she'd never kissed him before. She'd wondered so many times what that would feel like, but now the soft music and closeness intensified her curiosity. If she moved her face an inch closer to him, their lips would touch. It took every bit of strength within her to resist the impulse to do that.

She studied him as they danced. His dark hair looked like it could use a trimming, but she liked it full. His sideburns also looked like they could use a trimming, but she liked them long. His high cheek bones set off the beauty mark near his right eye, and the beauty mark set off his spectacular eyes.

Maxi's eyes were the most beautiful that she'd ever seen—jet black with deep-set brandy-brown flecks. They were mystical, mesmerizing, seductive, and even a little sinister—but they never frightened her.

Moreover, she detected a touch of sadness in them. She wondered what that was about and guessed that it had to do with losing his wife five years ago, or maybe feeling ashamed about the way he'd treated Felicity. Or maybe it didn't have to do with any past heart-wrenching experience at all, but it was just the way his eyes naturally looked. That lost-little-boy look went straight to her heart and made her want to reach out to him so badly that it drove her crazy to think she'd been keeping her love for him bottled up for the past four years.

"You're not such a bad dancer, Maxi."

He smiled. "Thanks, Jule." They were quiet again for a minute. "You're wearing a different scent than the one from this morning, aren't you?"

"This one is lavender."

"Very nice," he said. "You should sell lotions and perfumes here."

"Delilah was thinking about that."

"Where is Delilah?" he asked. "Cassandra said she hasn't seen her here in weeks."

"She's on vacation. You know, I guess this town really *has* been dead these past few weeks, especially Clover Lane. I wonder why."

"There are lots of events going on right now, Jule. The Monet exhibit at the museum in Philly. The auto show. And since the weather's getting warmer, I'm sure some people are heading to the shore. I like when it's quiet like this. It gives you a chance to think."

"Oh? What do you think about?"

He averted his eyes and blushed like he was embarrassed, which made her even more curious. Then he looked back at her and asked, "Did you ever draw Richard?"

She was a little surprised by the question. "That's what you think about?"

"Only because we were talking about your drawings just now."

She nodded, realizing that he wasn't going to tell her what kinds of things he *really* thought about, so she decided to drop the subject. "No, I never drew him."

"Jule, I'm sorry we haven't talked much these past few weeks."

"I think after what happened at the cemetery with Vienna, we've just been feeling awkward around each other. I'm so sorry that she hit you."

"It wasn't your fault," he said.

"Thank you for coming that day, Maxi. Having you there helped me very much."

"I'm glad, Jule."

She closed her eyes and rested her head on his shoulder, wondering whether she would ever get the chance to give her virginity to him. For almost four years he had owned her heart, but she didn't know how to tell him—or whether she even should. Vienna would be livid, Cassandra would hate seeing her friend date her dad, and Romy would disapprove because of the age difference. But the real problem was that she didn't know whether he loved her, too.

He slowly pulled away from her. "I'm sorry, Juliet, but I have to go."

He didn't say why. He just looked at her quietly for a moment, then he moved close to her very slowly and kissed her. The kiss was not passionate. It was brief and tender, an introductory kiss. A get-ready-for-more kiss that touched every part of her body in a sexual way. His lips were warm, and when he drew away from her, the air felt cold against her lips. She wanted that warmth back, but he turned and walked out the door as though nothing had happened.

She watched him leave, her breath coming slow and heavy. The silver bell over the doorway tinkled as he walked out. She closed her eyes and tried to regain her composure as she fondled the gold heart locket around her neck.

CHAPTER FOUR

"Did I wake you, Juliet?"

"No, Maxi, I was just watching TV in bed. Come on in."

He stepped into her living room. She wondered why in the world he would ring her doorbell at midnight, not that she minded. If he knocked on her door at three in the morning and woke her out of a dead sleep, she wouldn't be able to get to the door fast enough. He had changed into a black shirt and tan slacks. She'd always found him especially sexy in black.

"What are you watching?" he asked.

"Some steamy romantic thriller on one of the cable channels."

He smiled. "You don't seem like the type who likes steamy movies, but I guess deep down I always knew there was a beast inside of you, dying to come out."

She laughed. He looked her over in her mega-short, lacy pink nightgown with spaghetti straps and imprints of hearts scattered throughout.

"Do you always answer the door wearing skimpy lingerie?"

"You see more skin on a girl in a bikini," she said. "Besides, it's so warm out tonight."

She extended her arm to turn on the torch lamp in the corner of the living room, at the bottom of the stairs, but he touched her arm to stop her.

"If you don't mind, I'd rather you leave it off," he said.

"Why? Did you have a run-in with Vienna? Oh, Maxi, did she give you a black eye?"

She touched the skin near his eyes. The milky white moonlight that poured in through the windows played off of the curves of his face. His eyes glimmered in the charcoal grey of night. She couldn't make out the condition of his face very well for the shadows.

"No, it's nothing like that, Jule. I just like the dark. Some people think it's scary, but I think it's comforting and mystical. It's life-affirming."

"Life-affirming?"

"Well, just think about all of the lively things that happen in the dark," he said. "People have sweet dreams, sex dreams, nightmares, and hundreds of other kinds of dreams. Insomniacs toss and turn in the dark. Couples make love in the dark. They conceive children."

She smiled faintly. "So *those* are the kinds of things you think about."

Her gold heart locket must have caught the light, since his eyes rested on it.

"You always wear that," he said. "It's very beautiful. Is there a photo in it?"

"No," she lied. "It's just a locket I bought myself when I graduated high school." She didn't know how he would react if she told him that she was carrying his picture close to her heart. "Would you like a drink or something?"

"No, thanks, Jule."

The moonlight dappled across the living room floor and over the furniture in a way that reminded Juliet of a glittering silver ball in a disco nightclub.

"I guess you feel awkward being at home," she said, "since Vienna is staying there tonight."

"That isn't why I'm here. I just wanted to see you."

"So, Maxi, why won't you let me into your Shakespeare class?"

"I can't, Juliet. Let's just leave it at that."

She found it odd that he dismissed the subject so quickly. "Some day you're going to teach me something, even if it isn't Shakespeare." She smiled. "And even if it isn't in the classroom."

"I am? And just what am I going to teach you about?"

"Life," she said.

To Juliet, there was something so sexy about an older man. She felt that seductive power whenever she was in the same room with Maxi, and it wasn't because of his charm or his handsome face. It was all about the mystique and allure of a world that was unknown to her. He was experienced in matters of the heart, and something told her that he knew a little more than the average man about what women wanted—in and out of bed. The savageness in his soulful eyes was tempered with enough tenderness to tell her that he would be a patient but passionate lover if he took a virgin to bed. She yearned to know everything that he could teach her about the ways of the world and the kind of strength it took to survive in it.

"I'm no expert on life, Jule."

"Of course you are. You're Maxi Ward."

He smiled and brushed his hand over her cheek. "You are so beautiful," he whispered.

It was the first time he called her that. All her life, people had told her she was beautiful enough to be a model or a movie star, and that her statuesque five-foot-nine physique made her appear elegant and mature beyond her years. When she was in high school, her classmates were always telling her that she looked like a woman of twenty-three or four. Now, people she met at the boutique were shocked to learn that she was only twenty. Some of them thought that she was a married woman in her late twenties with a couple of children.

But in spite of all those compliments, the one person she'd always wanted praise from had never given her any until now. She felt like a veteran actress who'd finally won an Oscar and was too shocked to believe it. She smiled shyly.

"Thank you, Maxi."

His eyes looked like two flickering flashes of candlelight as he gazed at her. "I want to make love to you, Juliet, in a way that most people wouldn't even dare to fantasize about because it's so far out of their reach, they figure why bother?"

Her heartbeat accelerated. "Is that the real reason why you're here?"

He lowered his eyes secretively. He hid so much behind those beautiful eyes, so much that she was determined to uncover some day. She wanted to know the real Maxi Ward.

Finally, he looked up at her and said, "What does it matter? Something tells me you're going to wait until you're married. You seem like that kind of girl." He chuckled. "You want to hear a funny story about my wedding night?"

"Wedding nights are supposed to be romantic, not funny."

"There was nothing romantic about this wedding night," he said. "See, my wife was a virgin, and I'd been with just one girl I knew in high school. My wife was very nervous, so I said, 'Honey, if you feel that way, you take the bed.' I spent the entire night sitting on the windowsill, looking out at the traffic, sighing and thinking, 'Here I am on my honeymoon . . .'"

Juliet smiled. "Aw, you poor frustrated man."

She envied Maxi's late wife more than any other woman in the world, because for fifteen years she had the honor of being Mrs. Maximilian Ward. He had belonged to her and no other woman. All those years she had the privilege of living with him, sharing the simple day-to-day joys of life with him, and making love with him. The mere thought of fifteen years of sex with Maxi made Juliet sweat with desire. And oh, the endless kinds of sex! Gentle sex, passionate sex, orgasmic sex, make up sex—the list was never-ending. But best of all, his wife had left behind her the living, breathing proof of their love— Cassandra.

"I know this is none of my business, Jule, and you don't have to tell me if you don't want to."

"What is it, Maxi?"

"Did Richard ever try to seduce you?"

She nodded. "Sometimes."

Maxi narrowed his eyes, as though he hadn't expected her to say yes. "How hard did he try?"

"As hard as any typical teenage guy. He didn't hurt me or go too far with me."

"I hope not," he said, his dark eyes blazing furiously. "If he did, I'll kill him!"

She smiled and planted a generous kiss on his cheek. "Thank you for being so concerned about me, Maxi," she said tenderly.

His eyes twinkled with pride, which told her that the kiss had boosted his male ego. She was amazed at how much he made her feel like a woman even though they'd never made love, and that made her wonder just how much more womanly she would feel if they *did* make love.

"I didn't love Richard, Maxi." She looked deeply into his eyes. "You know that."

"It wasn't the right time for us back then, Jule. You were still in school. But I have to confess that I used to entertain thoughts about renting an apartment for us in Philly. I lived there when I was a kid. Did you know that? My family lived in a little row house in South Philly on Passyunk Avenue. We used to go to Pat's Steaks all the time. During the summer, we'd get Italian water ice and go for a stroll on Penn's Landing. Those were fun times. Then when I turned fourteen, my dad got a better job here in Tiger Lily, and the rest is history."

Juliet smiled. "You, Maxi? A city boy?"

"Surprise, surprise. So if we had rented an apartment, I would have taken you to Rittenhouse Square, the neighborhood Italian restaurants, and I'd have shown you the house I grew up in."

"And I would have painted you. That would have been great, Maxi. I would have rather taken a chance with you in secret than date Richard in public." She smiled faintly. "Maybe if I had, then it wouldn't have taken you four years to kiss me."

"I tried to kiss you at Christmas time, under the mistletoe, but you pushed me away."

"Vienna was in the other room, Maxi. I was afraid she'd walk in on us and give us grief."

He shook his head. "You're so afraid of what she thinks, aren't you?"

"No, I was just waiting for a time when we would be alone. And tonight at the boutique, it was perfect. It was worth waiting for." She smiled warmly. "You're not the only one who's entertained thoughts about us." She took his hand and moved in close to him. "I don't know what gives you the impression that I'm saving myself for marriage."

He looked offended by her attempt at seduction. "You want me to teach you about life, Jule? Here's lesson one: if you want to make love to a man, just come right out and tell him. Be a woman. And here's lesson two: be your *own* woman. Stop letting your sister control your life!"

She glowered at him. "Let me tell you something, you infuriating son of a bitch. If I really did let my sister control my life, then I would have thrown your ass out the door by now. And furthermore, if you have any doubts about my capabilities as a woman, then you might as well go screw yourself—because you'll never get to screw *me*!"

He stood back and threw her a look of surprise. "You're talking like Vienna, Jule. That doesn't become you. Maybe that's the beast inside of you that's been dying to come out." He looked her over with disappointment in his eyes. "And it's an ugly beast, too."

"Shut up, Maxi. Just get out of here."

"By the way, I don't want to screw you, Jule. I want to make love to you—or at least I did."

He stormed out the door. The screeching of the screen door echoed the screaming voices that attacked her brain. How could she say those awful things to the man who'd been a friend, father figure, and the love of her life all at once? She jogged after him as he strode angrily across the front lawn. The grass was warm against her bare feet. The moon shone in his dark hair, bringing out honey-brown highlights that she'd never noticed before. They matched the beautiful brandy-brown flecks in his eyes. With every passing day and every new moment that she and Maxi shared, she became more and more attracted to him—even after four years.

He stopped and turned to face her after he heard her feet smacking against the grass. She threw her arms around him. The second their bodies became fused together, they kissed hungrily. Suddenly all the anger between them melted away, and she forgot why she was angry at him in the first place. His lips were not full, the way many women loved men's lips, but his hot kiss was unlike any she'd ever felt before. She moaned sweetly as she tasted the fruity residue of wine on his lips and along the inside of his mouth. She kneaded her fingers over the muscles in his shoulders and upper back. He pulled her closer, his hands moving down her waist and squeezing her hips with an intensity that frightened and excited her at the same time.

"I'm sorry, Juliet. There's nothing ugly about you. You're the most beautiful woman I know."

"And you're my best friend, Maxi. You always look out for me. I—"

She stopped herself just before the words "I love you" came pouring out of her mouth.

"You what, Jule?"

She looked him straight in the eyes and took a deep, calm breath. Her mind was reeling from that incredible kiss that made her long for him like never before.

Finally she said, "I want to make love to you."

CHAPTER FIVE

She turned off the movie that she'd been watching in her bedroom. As he undressed, she closed the door and locked it in case Vienna came home from Cassandra's unexpectedly. She could tell that Maxi worked out in a gym a few times a week. His muscular body was so sexy that he put all the models and matinee idols to shame. They huddled together beneath the baby pink bedspread and pink sheet for a long time, tasting each other's kisses. She was still in her pink lace nightgown, because she wanted to give him the pleasure of taking it off. Until that moment, she'd never appreciated the hundreds of different ways a person can kiss. Maxi introduced her to every one of them. He teased her with kisses so achingly soft and quick that she barely felt them. He wowed her with gloriously long and lingering open-mouth kisses that allowed his tongue to flirt with hers. He ignited her lips with kisses that started out meek and tame but slowly turned mad and unstoppable. Maxi knew how to kiss her in ways that Richard never could or never even tried to. Her lips grew sore, but she didn't care. She relished the wonderful feeling of making up with Maxi after their first fight.

Just as he started to pull her spaghetti straps off her shoulders, she bit his lower lip in a moment of passion. He winced and sat up in bed with his fingers on his mouth.

"Oh, Maxi, I'm sorry!" She sat up, too, and tried to heal his injured lip with a light kiss. "I couldn't help myself. You're such a handsome man."

He looked surprised by the compliment. "It's been a long time since a woman has told me that," he said a little shyly.

"I find that extremely hard to believe."

The insecure, introverted look on his face somehow made his eyes look even more captivating than usual. They glowed with a pureness of heart that she'd never noticed before, and that elevated her feelings for him to a whole new plane. She nuzzled her nose against his and kissed the beauty mark near his right eye.

"You have the most beautiful eyes, Maxi. I've always wanted to tell you that."

He held her close and thanked her. He breathed in the floral scent of her long blond hair and moaned pleasurably as he exhaled. "Please forgive me, Juliet," he whispered. "You're such a sweet girl."

"Forgive you for what?"

"For wanting to make love to you as badly as I do," he said.

She smiled slightly. "Then maybe I should apologize to you for the same thing."

They fell into each other's arms and kissed again. He pulled the spaghetti straps off her shoulders and all the way down her arms. The pink and white heart-speckled Tiffany lamp by her bed was still on, so when the nightgown finally slid off her torso, his eyes lit up when he saw her huge breasts. She pulled off the nightgown completely as he stared at her bosom. He looked awestruck, as though he'd never seen breasts so voluptuous. She'd always considered hers to be a curse. They were the first thing that men noticed about her. Maxi had always been the exception. Every time he laid his eyes on her, they were meeting her own eyes. If he *had* noticed her breasts, he did a fabulous job of pretending like they weren't the first or the only thing that he noticed about her.

But now that she sat naked in front of him, she saw that he couldn't hide his amazement and excitement anymore. Maxi the gentleman was gone. Male lust had chased him away. His eyes widened as though he'd uncovered buried treasure. He brushed his left hand over the side of her left breast in a counterclockwise motion while brushing his right hand over the side of her right breast in a clockwise motion. His hands slowly swept over the underside of her breasts before they gradually moved in towards the center and caressed the velvety smooth mounds, feeling all of their dimensions as though he'd never touched a woman's breasts before.

He bent over and kissed one of her pink nipples, and she instantly knew that he'd ensnared her once and for all. One light kiss on an intimate part of her body was all it took to make her see everything clearly. Whatever space she had put between her and Maxi for the past four years, it was now a thing of the past. No longer did she care what Vienna thought or Cassandra or Romy. She was his, completely. He gratified her again with another shy but scorching kiss just above her nipple. She lifted herself up and knelt before him so that her breasts would be at his eye level. He gratefully slid his arms around her and kissed every curve of her breasts in a slow and methodical fashion, putting great feeling into each kiss. She closed her eyes, and her head and neck dropped backward slightly as she fell harder and harder under the spell of those orgiastic kisses. He savored every kiss with a thankful moan that told her he was ecstatic to be a man. She rhythmically coursed her long fingers through the dark hair that she'd so longed to touch, and suddenly she realized how quickly everything had changed. The skittish, apologetic man who had entered her bedroom a minute ago was now kissing her breasts and nipples with unabashed, manic desire. His transformation dazzled her. She loved knowing that she had the power to bring out the red-blooded side of Maximilian Ward. Suddenly those big, arresting breasts didn't feel like a curse to her anymore.

A cool breeze wafted through the open window, gently blowing the sheer cotton-candy pink curtains as it massaged her skin with the allure of a lover's touch. "That feels so good," she whispered as she held his head and stroked his long sideburns with her thumbs. She breathed in the scent of his musk cologne, letting it go to her head and weaken her senses. "Maximilian . . ." Her voice sounded distant and trancelike, as though she was speaking in a dream.

He brushed his cheeks against her breasts. His coarse five o'clock shadow grazed her skin but didn't hurt her one bit. Instead it sent tingles of rapture all through her feminine flesh, seducing her by reminding her that he was a man in waiting. She loved being enveloped by that raw, steamy masculinity. It was the kind of manliness that challenged her and made her question whether she was woman enough for him, and she was more than eager to accept the challenge.

He sucked on her nipples like a man who hadn't been alone with a woman in years and was now making up for lost time. The warmth of his tongue and the inner flesh of his mouth against her nipples made her heave her chest with even greater desire, and that encouraged him to open his mouth wider and suck even more deeply. She pulled him closer and buried her face in the thicket of his hair as she heaved her chest again. Her flowing blond tresses hung near the sides of his face like gold satin ribbons, caressing his cheeks as he kissed and sucked on her breasts. He ran his hand up her thigh with manly expertise, then he gingerly worked his fingers and thumb over her crotch while he continued to suck on her breasts. The combination of those three enticing acts revved up her juices to the maximum, leaving her so supercharged with sexual stimulation that she just couldn't stand all the foreplay anymore. He looked at her hungrily through a succession of urgent pants and drew her back until her head hit the pillow.

He pulled her pink lace panties down her long and shapely legs, kissing her thighs and calves as he did so. She loved the mad, carefree way that he flung her panties and nightgown off the bed. When he finally took her, she gasped in surprise over the enormous size of him inside her. She couldn't believe how gently and slowly he was entering her, considering the ravenous look in his eyes a moment ago. He let out a long, hushed breath of satisfaction after every thrust. His eyes were closed now. A dreamy look of peacefulness, relief, and sheer bliss came over his face. He looked like a man who was feeling the warmth of the sun for the very first time in months, maybe even years. Maybe he used to think that sweet girls like her were unattainable or extinct, and that entering her was like entering an exotic land that shimmered with all things good and untainted—a land he had once known but had left behind so many years ago. He held her close as he continued to penetrate her, kissing her face and her neck all over like a man who'd been deprived of female affection for an excruciatingly long time. She couldn't imagine that being the case. He was way too handsome. In her mind, he was ten times sexier than all of the Hollywood matinee idols put together—both living and dead. He was the only man she had ever made fantasy love to. As she laid beneath him, she couldn't believe that it wasn't a fantasy anymore.

"My Juliet," he whispered. "My baby girl . . ."

It was the first time he'd ever called her that. The instant she heard it, it rushed through her system like an addictive drug. Maybe it sounded like a juvenile pet name, but she knew that he didn't mean it that way. Sure, it glittered with sugar and innocence. But beneath that crystalline veneer, the name smoldered with sensuality and a swoon-inducing quality that didn't make her feel like a little girl at all.

He gazed down at her. Triumph glimmered serenely in his now docile eyes, and that subtle display of machismo aroused her. He kissed her lips in such a gentlemanly manner that she couldn't believe he'd just made love to her.

"Are you okay, Juliet?"

She smiled up at him, still feeling like her entire being hovered between reality and some fantastical dream world. "Yes, Maxi, I'm okay."

They made love for hours, keeping the light on so that he could see her body. His lips danced across her abdomen and stomach and then up and down the peaks of her breasts. He ran his hands over the crescent-shaped curves of her body with such masterful skill that she wriggled with feverish delight. His nostrils drank in the lavender scent of her skin while he dragged his tongue over her flesh and kissed her belly button and the dip in between her breasts. He tickled her ear with amorous whispers, calling her his ravishing lover as he nipped her earlobe while they had sex. When their eyes met, she saw so much fiery love in his scintillating orbs that she almost had to look away. The feeling was so intense. He sat up in bed with her and held her dearly from behind, kissing her shoulders and the sides of her neck and playfully biting her in spots. She pushed her hair aside and let it all hang over one shoulder so that he could kiss the back of her neck. Her insides went up in flames from the pressure of his bulging, rock-solid chest against the supple slope of her back as he gently rocked her in his arms and whispered "My beautiful Juliet." She turned to him, and they fell on the bed together and kissed desperately until her lips became sore again. He created an invisible zig-zag of kisses and tongue strokes on all of the beauty marks that spanned her body. He entered her again and again, wearing her out but making her hunger for more at the same time.

"Maximilian," she breathed as she gently dug her teeth into his shoulder and her fingernails into his back. "Please." She couldn't decide whether to say "Stop" or "Don't stop."

"I love the way you say my name," he murmured.

He kissed her neck voraciously as he continued to penetrate her. She pressed the crown of her head into the pillow as he kissed and licked the underside of her chin and brushed his chest against her breasts while they had intercourse. She felt him all over her and inside her, racing through her with a force so strong that it exploded inside her like fireworks. She shrieked excitedly, feeling like a current of electricity was shimmying through her bloodstream.

"Do you want me to stop?" he asked, his hot breath beating against her neck.

"No! Please don't stop."

But he did. He sat up in bed and let out a wild breath, like a football fan who'd just watched his favorite team win the Superbowl or an athlete who'd just undergone a vigorous but exhilarating workout at the gym. He wiped the sweat from his face and turned off the lamp.

"I'm sorry, baby girl." He drew her into the toasty warmth of his broad chest. "I'm exhausted."

"*You're* exhausted? A big, strong man like you? Oh, Maxi, come on." She kissed his neck and chest temptingly.

"Even big, strong men get exhausted from time to time, sweetheart."

She turned away in frustration and rested on her side. He draped his arm over her waist.

"Don't be mad at me," he pleaded quietly.

He sounded like a sad little boy. That was the side of him that always went straight to her heart. She quickly turned back to him and kissed him insanely.

"I'm not mad at you, Maxi."

She was mad *about* him. All he'd done was keep his promise. He'd said he wanted to make love to her in a way that most people wouldn't even dare to fantasize about.

As the saying went, always keep them wanting more.

"Was that your first time, sweetheart?" he asked.

"Yes, Maxi."

He took her hand and kissed the back of it. "Are you okay?"

"Yes." She smiled. "Thank you for asking me again."

His eyes shone like the ripples of black satin sheets as he looked at her. With his free hand, he brushed his fingertips over her lips. "So does my lovely tenderfoot feel any different?"

"Just overwhelmed, in an ecstatic way," she said.

He turned her hand over and kissed her fingertips in that same achingly soft way that he'd kissed her lips when they entered her bedroom. "Well, good night, Jule." He gave her a very deep and delectable good-night kiss, then he whispered, "Sweet dreams, baby girl."

She swallowed hard, fighting to suppress her sexual impulses. For a man who wasn't in the mood for seduction anymore, he was sure seducing the hell out of her. She said good night to him and closed her eyes. About ten seconds later, she heard him call her name. She opened her eyes, and in a smooth and deliciously sinful voice he said, "Do you want to make love again?"

"I thought you were exhausted."

He grinned devilishly and whispered, "I lied."

CHAPTER SIX

Maxi was still sleeping soundly when she awoke. It was still dark outside. The moon was faint but visible through the curtains. She glanced at the white digital clock on the wooden nightstand by her bed. The fluorescent green numbers read four A.M.

She watched the tranquil rise and fall of his chest as he slept. Trying not to wake him, she touched his face with her fingertips. His rough, unshaven skin felt like sandpaper. She brushed her fingertips over his lips. She swept her lips over his full eyelashes. They felt like feathers against her mouth. She kissed his eyelids, his cheek, and his forehead and caressed his dark hair just as he began to stir. His eyelashes flickered, but his eyes were still closed. She wondered whether he was dreaming and what kinds of things he dreamt about. She leaned over to kiss his lips just as he was opening his eyes, and her long hair smacked him in the eye. He let out a drowsy "Ow!"

"Maxi honey, I'm sorry." She kissed his eyelid again and then his lips.

"That's okay, Jule," he answered sleepily. He smiled through half opened eyes that looked like two slits. "So how are you, baby girl?" His voice was woozy and liquor-tinged, as though he'd been up all night drinking that fruity wine that she'd tasted in his kiss.

"Great, Maxi." She smiled. "Your voice is sexy when you're half asleep."

He propped his elbow on the pillow and rested his head against his hand. "And you are a breath-taking vision with your hair sprawled on the pillow like that." He laced his fingers through hers and gently squeezed her hand. "I'm glad I was your first, Jule. You're very special, and I don't think any man is good enough for you."

"You are, Maxi."

"No, I'm not. But thank you for saying so, sweetie."

She gazed at him, trying to picture a twenty-year-old Maxi. "I wish I'd known you when you were my age."

"You wouldn't have liked me very much. I skipped classes to go to strip joints and porno movies. I hit the bars and clubs way more times than I hit the books. Sometimes I snuck those mini bottles of liquor into class and took a swig when the teacher's back was turned."

"Oh, come on, Maxi. Romy said you were shy in school."

"I was shy in high school, but once I started college I opened up and had more fun."

"I'd love to hear about those times," she said.

"So would I. I don't remember most of them."

She laughed.

"No, really, I don't," he said. "That's how much fun I had. Too many hangovers and drunken nights that slipped my mind when I woke up the next day—at four in the afternoon."

"You couldn't have been that wild, Maxi. You got married shortly afterward, didn't you?"

"Yeah, at twenty-one. My wife and I had a whirlwind romance. She straightened me out and helped me to grow up."

"I want to know everything about you, Maxi. What inspired you to become a teacher, whether you were lonely growing up an only child—everything."

"How did you know I was an only child?"

"Cassandra told me," she said.

"Maybe you and I have more in common than we realized, Jule. You grew up with a sibling but no father. I grew up with a father but no siblings. We both missed out on something."

Suddenly the sadness in his eyes was starting to make more sense to her. She wanted to tell him that she loved him, but she was afraid that he might not say it back. Instead, she channeled all of that love into her actions. She dampened him with kisses down his neck and on his pectoral muscles and washboard abs, dragging her hair and her breasts over his skin. She straddled him and gently rocked her body to and fro, again and again, as she ran her fingers over the curves of his chest and through his dark chest hairs. Slowly she gathered her hair together and piled it loosely on top of her head as he cupped his hands on her breasts. Moving her body to the rhythm of his heavy breathing, she moaned as she felt him inside her, as his fingers tenderly probed her breasts. He closed his eyes, and in a sex-drenched whisper he uttered, "Oh, baby." She let go of her hair. It cascaded down her back as she laid her hands caressingly on the hands that were on her breasts and then slowly ran her hands over his hairy arms. His hands glided down her sides, over her hips, and up her back. He pulled her toward him, and they spent the next hour tumbling around on the bed together as they made love non-stop. When weariness finally overtook them and they stopped, her locket hit him in the eye.

"Oh, Maxi, I'm sorry!" She kissed him. "Are you okay?"

"I'll live." He held the locket in his fingers and kissed it. "Where did you learn how to make love like that?" He smiled. "Those steamy cable movies, I suppose."

She pulled the locket out of his grasp without answering him. He glared at her.

"Baby girl, are you in love with the mystery man whose picture you don't want me to see?"

"There's no other man, Maxi. I love *you*." She kissed him, feeling relieved and freer than ever now that it was finally out in the open. "I love you."

He said nothing, as though he wasn't sure he heard her right and was trying to mentally process her words. When he finally did speak, his voice sounded sad.

"Believe me, sweetheart, one day I'll just be a distant memory in your mind."

"Maxi, you wouldn't say that if you knew how much I've loved you all these years." She kissed him again, wanting so desperately to take away that sadness. Tears of joy filled her eyes. Twenty-four hours ago, she had no idea what it felt like to kiss him on the lips. Since then, they'd shared hundreds of kisses. They'd made love again and again, and he still hadn't left her bed. "All these years I was afraid to say it, Maxi, but why should that be? I have nothing to be ashamed of. I'm deliriously in love with you, and I don't care what Vienna thinks. I did let her get in the way before, and I'm sorry. I promise you I'll never let that happen again."

"It's not Vienna, Jule. Some day you're going to meet another man, and he's going to take you away from me. I'll hate it, and I'll hate him for doing it. But I'll be powerless to stop it. He's going to show you what the rest of the world is like, outside of this small town. He's the one who will teach you about life, not me. He'll whisk you off to New York or Los Angeles or who knows where. You'll become a world-famous artist, and when I visit galleries and museums and see your work on display, I'll say to myself, 'I remember a time when that darling girl was mine.' And you'll look back on our time together, and you'll remember me simply as the man who gave you your first taste of love and helped turn you into a woman."

"I don't give a damn about other men, Maxi. I think every other man in the world is ugly next to you, even the movie stars. Every single time I kissed Richard, I was kissing you in my mind. Believe me, I'm exactly where I want to be right now. No other man will ever take me away from you." She smiled and took him in her arms. "Come make love to your baby girl."

He obeyed without hesitation. She couldn't believe that Vienna actually thought this man was a rapist. A rapist could never speak so sensitively to a young woman in love. He could never kiss and fondle her breasts as tenderly as Maxi did. He could never look lovingly in her eyes while they were having sex. No, Maxi couldn't have raped Felicity.

"No," she moaned. "No!"

He sat up in bed with the springiness of a jack-in-the-box, looking confused. "No?"

She threw her arms around him. "I'm sorry, honey. I didn't mean it that way. I was thinking out loud about something else."

He looked at her sorely. "While we were making love?"

"You're not the terrible person Vienna thinks you are. That's what I was thinking about. Maxi, you've given me the most wonderful night of my life, not because you made me a woman but because *you* made me a woman." She kissed him sincerely. "I love you," she whispered, wishing with all of her heart that he would say it back to her, hoping that her words and actions would stir up something inside him that would make him say it.

But he didn't. He just gazed at her intimately, and she saw in his eyes that he felt it. She could tell that he wanted to say it, but something was holding him back. He drew her near and kissed *her* this time, and they sunk onto the bed and made love again.

CHAPTER SEVEN

Juliet came bounding down the stairs like a little girl who'd just received a roomful of teddy bears for her birthday. She hugged Vienna and Cassandra.

"I love you guys," she said in a musical voice. "You're the best friends and the best sisters. Cass, I'll pretend that you're my sister, too, okay?"

"Are you all right, Jule?" Vienna asked. "Your lip looks bruised."

"Oh, it's nothing. It's just a little sore."

Vienna knew that something weird was going on, and it could only mean one thing—Maxi.

She sighed and collapsed on the floral-patterned white sofa, burying her face into a white, heart-shaped pillow that Juliet had made in her senior-year sewing class. She squeezed the pillow tightly, feeling like the *Peanuts* character Linus with his security blanket.

"What's wrong, Vienna?" Cassandra asked as she sat beside her.

"This has your old man written all over it, Cass, and we don't have time for it. You have to get to school, and I have to get to my ten-fifteen interview at the CPA firm."

"Isn't it funny that my dad and I both have first period free on Friday?" Cassandra said.

"Yeah, but he usually gets there when school starts and he works at his desk, right?"

"Not today," Cassandra said. "He came home a little while ago, before you and I left my place and came here. Didn't you see him?"

"No, I must have been in your bathroom." Vienna looked at her curiously. "Where was he all night?"

"Look, I'm wearing his dress!" Juliet cried. She spun around in her ankle-length, body-hugging ivory dress with the slit up one side.

"Maxi gave you that dress?" Vienna asked.

"No, he just likes it." Juliet ran a silver Victorian-style, heart-shaped brush over her long blond hair as she peered in the oval beveled mirror in the living room and sighed happily. "Today feels like a special day." She stuffed the brush back in her beige leather purse and then pulled out a gold tube of lipstick. "He came by the boutique last night," she said as she dabbed a touch of frosted pink lipstick on her naked lips. "We slow-danced to 'Ebb Tide,' and we talked for a while. It was like a regular date." She straightened the locket around her neck and lovingly laid it dead-center over her skin. "Oh, Cass, I don't know how you can stand living with him day in and day out with your bedroom just a few feet away from his. Don't you ever wonder what it would feel like to make love to him?"

"He's her father!" Vienna cried.

"Well, some girls have very handsome fathers."

"But they don't want to go to bed with them, Jules!"

"Maybe some of them do. What do we know? There's a term for girls like that. They have an Electra complex."

"I don't have that at all," Cassandra told her. "Even if my dad *is* handsome."

"God, Jules, I'm starting to feel grateful that we never knew our father," Vienna said. "You probably would have had sex fantasies about him. Hell, maybe you already do. Maybe deep down, you think Maxi's our father."

"No, I don't." She chuckled. "He better not be, after what we did last night."

Vienna's heart was pounding furiously. Suddenly she felt like a scary scene from a horror movie was unfolding right before her eyes.

"Oh, my God," she muttered, rolling her eyes in disgust.

"Forget I said that, Vien."

"You had sex with him, didn't you? Did he hurt you? Is that why your lip looks bruised?"

"We kissed a lot. It got pretty heated, and we bit each other a few times by accident." Juliet turned to Cassandra. "Cass, it's true. I slept with your father last night." She blushed and smiled shyly. "Although we didn't get much sleep."

Vienna shrieked, sounding a lot like one of those horror movie victims as she scrambled out of her curled up position on the sofa and jumped to her feet. As Juliet tucked her hair behind her ears, Vienna noticed little bites on the sides of her neck and on her shoulders.

"My God, the man is an animal! Jules, how could you do this to Mom?"

"Vienna, I know you don't want to accept this, but I love him very much. I'm not built like you—hard, tough, and unforgiving. I see a side to him that you don't see. He gets inside of me, all the time. When I see him, when I don't see him—it doesn't matter. He's there! And he loves me, too. He didn't tell me, but I know he does." She looked down at the carpet like she was reflecting on this. "I hadn't thought about this at first. I forgot it happened, but now it flashed in my mind again."

"What's that?" Vienna asked.

"While we were having sex, he asked me if I was okay, as though he wanted to make sure he wasn't hurting me." She smiled softly. "He was very gentle, maybe even gentler than most women would want a man to be."

Vienna shook her head. "Honestly, Jules, I don't know what the hell goes through your mind, making love with a man who used to hit our mother." She fixed Juliet's hair so that it covered the love bites. "You can't let the customers see that."

"I told you, he's not the same man he was two years ago. How can you keep bringing this up in front of Cassandra?"

"That's okay, Jule," Cassandra said. "It doesn't bother me anymore. Listen, it's been five years since my mom died. Something or someone needs to brighten up his life again. If you're that someone, then I'm happy for you both."

"Thank you, Cass." Juliet embraced her. "You're a saint. Nothing ever seems to bother you." She looked at Vienna. "You could take a lesson from her, sis. Cass, you're going to make a great doctor some day. With that calm, relaxed attitude you'll always put your patients at ease. You're going to be a real asset to the medical community. Listen, I've got to run or I'll be late for work. Good luck on your interviews,

Vien. Call me at the boutique if you get an offer. We'll go out this weekend and celebrate, my treat. All three of us."

"I'm up for that," Cassandra said. "See you, Jule."

Juliet headed out the door. Vienna tried to forget about Maxi and Juliet by turning her attention to the ferns and spider plants in the vestibule and on the coffee table, checking the soil for dryness.

"You know, Vien, I'm not really happy about this either," Cassandra said, "but I love them both, so I'm trying to be supportive." She laid a hand on Vienna's shoulder. "Say, let's do something again tonight. Get our minds off of this."

"Cass, you should hate me for hating your dad," Vienna said as she shot a few mists of water at the ferns with her plastic spray bottle. "Why don't you?"

"Because you're bold and direct, never afraid to speak your mind, no matter what anyone thinks. I love you, Vien. I want to be like you some day."

"God help you, Cass!"

"You know, Vienna, maybe you need to find someone to love, too. Maybe *that* would take your mind off of this."

Vienna chuckled. "Yeah, that'll be the day."

"That you find someone or that it'll take your mind off of Jule and my dad?"

"Both," Vienna said as she watered the spider plants and inspected the leaves for brown spots.

"Still, I think you need someone who will love you no matter what."

"Whatever, Cass."

"Don't you *want* to find someone?"

That seemed like a strange question to Vienna. She'd never really thought about it before. "I don't know. I think all that happiness would make me feel like I'm going to explode. Happiness overkill, if that's possible."

Cassandra nodded. "And you already feel like you're going to explode, because my dad drives you crazy. You know, Vien, it amazes me that you've managed to pull a 4.0 every semester for the past three years at Columbia in spite of that whole nightmare with him."

"I think it's my anger that drives me. But I'll admit, I shouldn't have hit him right there at the cemetery, at my own mother's funeral.

I guess that makes me a hypocrite for criticizing him, but I'm not a man hitting a woman. I only did that because I was looking out for Jules."

"I really admire the way you try to protect your sister," Cassandra said.

"Let's not talk about me anymore. What about you? Maybe *you* need to find someone."

Cassandra smiled faintly, almost mysteriously. "I don't think that's going to be a problem for me."

CHAPTER EIGHT

"Why, hello, Vienna." Maxi looked at his watch. "A quarter to four." He shook his head. "You're late. I figured you'd get here the minute I got home from school—three-fifteen sharp."

Two seconds after Vienna stepped into his living room, she socked him in the nose. He stumbled backward a few steps and put his hand up to his bloody nostrils.

"I figured you'd do that, too," he said as he pulled a wad of tissues out of his pocket and pressed them against his nose. A few drops of blood cascaded down his sky blue T-shirt, creating purple stains.

"What the hell are you doing, Maxi, screwing around with my sister?"

He smiled. "Ferns and spider plants are too delicate for you, Vienna. With that prickly personality of yours, you seem more like a cactus kind of gal." He eyed her in her black blazer and matching skirt. "Why are you all dressed up?"

"I had a couple of job interviews today."

"How'd they go?" he asked.

"Don't change the subject, Maxi. Just stay away from my sister."

"I won't do that, for you or anyone else." He checked his blue jeans for blood stains but found none. "Gotta throw my shirt in the laundry now, thanks to your animalistic behavior."

"You're the wild animal on this block, Maxi, not me. I saw those love bites you left on Jules' neck and shoulders. I'm afraid to see what the hell you did to the rest of her body. My God, there are enough bites on that poor girl to make even a vampire nauseous!"

"I didn't hear any complaints from Juliet last night. Besides, I will not apologize to you for being a passionate lover."

He pulled his shirt over his head, messing up his hair a little, and threw the shirt on the dark blue leather couch. He stood in his pants and a sleeveless white undershirt. His biceps bulged as he folded his hairy arms across his chest. Suddenly Vienna felt distracted and a little uneasy.

"Don't you want to put on another shirt?" she asked as she awkwardly averted her eyes and disinterestedly looked at some of the objects that decorated the living room. First her eyes rested on an Austrian crystal bowl in the center of the cherry wooden coffee table. Then they jumped up to the pewter-framed photos of Cassandra and Maxi that were perched on the mantel.

"Yes, I do, if you would please leave."

"I'm not going anywhere," she said, looking back at him with a scowl. "You know, Maxi, for years I was afraid this would happen. But deep down I guess I was a little stupid and naïve to think that just maybe you could restrain yourself. Or maybe you'd wise up, do the right thing, and tell her you're not the right man for her. You know Jule. She's a sweet, starry-eyed girl. She's emotionally fragile and vulnerable, because she can't get over the fact that she grew up without a father. And that's where you come in, Maxi. You know she thinks of you as her safety net, but you also know that you're no damn good for her! So what the hell are you doing with her? Please, let her go, otherwise she'll never bring this father fixation to a close."

"I'm not letting her go, Vienna. You may not believe this, but I love your sister."

"Then why didn't you tell her that last night?"

"Because I think she's going to meet another man some day."

"Another man? What the hell! Maxi, you're all she thinks about. She's been giving you those wistful, lovey-dovey looks for the past three and a half years. In case it hasn't registered in your brain, she's in love with you! Last night was her first time."

"I know, she told me. She told me everything."

Vienna gasped. "You sleazy son of a bitch! She saved herself for you. You devirginized her. She told you she loves you, and you didn't say it back even though you claim to love her, too?"

"I didn't mean to hurt her. I'll straighten everything out with her, don't worry."

"You can't give her the kind of love she needs, Maxi. My sister is the kind of girl who wants to be *showered* with love. Think Niagara Falls. Think rain storms that leave you soaking wet to the point where your clothes are sticking to your skin. She wants soulmate love that lasts forever. I'm talking serious stuff here, Maxi. No games and no one-night stands. So if you can't deliver, then you'd best get the hell out right now, before any serious damage is done."

"Vienna, let me tell you how my feelings for Juliet have evolved over the years. When I first became attracted to her, when she was a teenager, I didn't really know whether I loved her. I was just starting to get over my wife's death. Jule was so sweet and mysterious to me. I guess in my mind, she was too beautiful to be a virgin, but at the same time she exuded sensuality without acting overtly sexy. She had class and elegance. She seemed to walk this fine line between fantasy girl and the girl next door, and it drove me crazy!"

"I see, Maxi. You wanted her, but if you got her in bed, that would kill her good-girl image."

"Right, and there was something very awe-inspiring about that image. It seemed a shame to tamper with it. But as I became more deeply attracted to her, I realized that I didn't think of her as a teenager. In many ways I never treated her that way either. Even now I sometimes forget that she's only twenty, because she looks so much older. There's something celestial and radiant about her. She has an openness and honesty that's so rare in people nowadays. And she actually sees good in me! That's something that I haven't been able to see in a very long time."

"Maxi, if you ever hurt her the way you hurt my mother, I'm going to send you straight to an early grave."

He looked at her with a trace of a silly smile. "You know, Vienna, I can't help but wonder whether all of your hostility toward me is masking sexual frustration. I saw the way you looked at me when I took off my shirt. I noticed the mixture of uneasiness and arousal in your eyes."

She laughed. "Arousal! Yeah, that'll be the day."

He pulled his undershirt over his head.

"Maxi!" She backed away from him while she eyed his pectoral muscles and chest hair.

He tossed the undershirt on the couch over his T-shirt, then he moved close to her, backing her up against the front door. Something was swimming around in the back of his dark eyes as he studied her carefully. It looked like a bizarre blend of flirtation, suspicion, amusement, and an inflated male ego.

Finally he said, "Are you angry at me because I made love to Juliet last night instead of you? Is that what this is all about? Jealousy?"

"I bet you'd *like* me to feel jealous. I bet that would make you feel like a real man, getting both the Mann girls all worked up and hot for you."

He took her in his arms and kissed her full on the lips. She shoved him in the chest and wiped her mouth with the back of her hand.

"Where the hell do you get off?" she hissed.

"You've always got some smart-ass answer to everything, don't you? You need a man to come along and shut you the hell up. If kissing you is the only way to do it, then hell, I'm willing to give it a try. Besides, you *wanted* me to kiss you. The second you found out I slept with Juliet, you rushed over here, pretending to be concerned for her well-being. But that's just a smokescreen, isn't it? Code language for 'Maxi, I want you myself.' Up until now, it never occurred to me that you might actually view her as competition. I don't know why it took me this long to figure it out, but that's got to be the answer. It's the only thing that makes sense. After all, you *are* a woman. I guess I have a tendency to forget that."

"You're crazy, Maxi! Maybe you want *me*. Maybe you want to do a little one-on-one time with me up in your bedroom right now, and then tonight get me and Jules together for some three-way action back at my place."

He kissed her again, and again she pushed him away, slapping him hard across the face.

"Kissing me is not going to shut me up, Maxi."

"You're a wild animal that needs to be tamed, and your imagination is seriously polluted."

"And you're the last man on earth I want to kiss," she said. "God, you are so egotistical! You must think you're saturated with sex appeal— the lusty Lothario of Tiger Lily. Isn't it enough that you've got one Mann sister under your spell? Can't you be satisfied with that?"

"I'll be satisfied when you show me that you're woman enough to admit the truth—that you're attracted to me on some level. I bet your heart's fluttering like a butterfly right now, because you're finally seeing me as a man. Not as the guy who hit your mother or slept with your sister, but a *man*. And you don't know how the hell to deal with that. You want to turn and run."

"You don't know the first thing about me, Maxi—or about how to treat a woman."

"You don't *act* like a woman. You act like a vicious rain storm that never lets up. A snarling, growling dog that never stops barking or flashing his fangs. You don't know how to act like a woman. And it's a shame, because you're beautiful. You're Juliet's twin, after all. You've got all the right stuff. Too bad you don't know how to use it to your advantage. I bet you scare away all those college men at Columbia, don't you? I bet you get a huge thrill, shoving them around and pretending you're one of them."

She smacked his face again.

"Hitting me is your demented way of showing me affection, isn't it, Vienna?"

"What would you rather I do, Maxi? Slither out of my clothes and throw myself at you?"

"No, but if that's what you really want to do, why don't you just say so?"

"Get over yourself, Maxi. Contrary to what you may think, not every woman in Tiger Lily is dying to get in your pants. Believe me, I didn't come here because I secretly love being alone with you, and I didn't come here to get kissed by you. I'm worried about Jules, and you are the cause of my worries. You've *been* the cause of my worries for years. I'm not harboring tawdry, paperback-romance feelings of desire for you. *I hate you!* I hate what you did to my mother, and I hate whatever you did to my sister to make her fall in love with you. I hate that my mother is dead and you're still here. And I hate you for infesting my heart with so much damn hatred that I don't know how to function like a normal, happy, mentally stable human being anymore!"

She turned to leave.

"I'm sorry, Vienna, for everything. Really, I wouldn't say that if I didn't mean it. I know it doesn't take away what I did, and if I could bring Felicity back—for both you and Juliet—I swear I would. You know

I made peace with her long before she died, and I'd like to make peace with you, too."

His voice washed over her with a gentleness that she'd never felt before. She turned around and faced him again. His eyes were calmly and sweetly beckoning her, pleading with her to forgive him.

"Will you at least think about it?" he asked, keeping his voice at a feather-soft pitch. For the first time, it actually sounded sexy to her—which made her cringe. She wouldn't have any of that with him.

"Whatever, Maxi." She expelled a nervous breath, trying not to look at his muscular physique but finding it virtually impossible to shift her eyes away from it.

"Are you all right?"

"I'm fine," she said.

"Are you sure?"

"Yes."

Now her own voice was silky soft, and she suddenly realized that she was flirting with *him.* His eyes met hers. He held the look for a minute, then he moved toward her very slowly and kissed her on the lips. This time his kiss was not forceful. It was timid and virginal, and its softness tempted her somehow. It made her want more. She wouldn't kiss him back, but she didn't push him away either. She was starting to feel afraid now. Strange feelings were starting to well up inside her, feelings that she wanted to feel for some other man. He started to kiss her neck. She closed her eyes. The feelings were getting stronger and dirtier, and she could feel herself slip away. She knew he was only testing her, trying to see whether she was woman enough to respond to a man's advances. But with every second that passed, she found herself caring less about his motives. She began to feel hot. She didn't know whether it was because she was standing so close to the devil incarnate, or if it was actually possible that she was enjoying his little game. Her breath came heavy as he continued to kiss her neck. She knew she should have stopped him, but she couldn't think straight. All she could do was feel. She began to wonder what it would feel like to kiss him back, and deep down some trashy little part of her was hoping that he would kiss her again on the lips so that she could find out. And it was almost as though he knew that, because the next thing he did was kiss the corners of her mouth without touching her lips. She tried to kiss his mouth a few times, but he jerked away from her, leaving just a hairline of space between their faces. It was like he was playing a game with her, teasing her, and that made her want him even more.

He let her have one soft kiss, which she immediately responded to, and then he pulled away from her. He indulged her a second time, letting the kiss last just a little longer before pulling away yet again. His eyes were sultry but cool somehow, and they were still beckoning her. Daring her. She was starting to get a glimpse into that dark, lurid, and sexy world that Juliet found so bewitching.

Finally, he took Vienna in his arms and gave her the passionate kiss that she wanted. She wrapped her arms around his broad shoulders and reveled in the tautness of his muscles. His arms were powerful against her small frame, and that magnificent strength excited her. For a minute, she actually forgot who she was kissing. She liked letting go of herself, losing control, and feeling uninhibited. She liked feeling his fingers comb through her hair while his tongue brushed against hers. She loved discovering another side of herself, one that had nothing to do with yelling, threatening, or punching.

When the kiss ended, she opened her eyes and saw smudges of her red lipstick all over his mouth. Suddenly her cheeks felt like two fireballs. She lowered her eyes in shame, unable to believe that she'd just kissed Maxi Ward.

"Well, what do you know?" he said. "I always wondered whether there was a real, live flesh and blood woman hiding deep down inside there, dying to come out. I sure got my answer."

She hurriedly turned to leave when he laid a hand on her arm. She spun around defensively.

"Get away from me!" she cried.

"I'm not going to kiss you again, I promise. I'm sorry, Vienna. I was trying to prove a point and I got a little carried away." He smiled softly. "Who would have thought I'd actually enjoy kissing you?"

"Maxi—"

"Relax. I'm in love with Juliet. I just think you're a great kisser. I guess I should have known you'd be, since you're a passionate person. Maybe you should turn that passionate energy in another direction from now on, and use it for love instead of hate." He paused a second with an expression of mild chagrin on his face. "Maybe I shouldn't say this, but I think underneath all our bickering and hollering, you and

I have some kind of weird chemistry. Maybe it's *because* of the bickering and hollering."

"Come on, Maxi—"

"It's just an observation." He looked directly in her eyes. "I love Juliet, Vienna. If you don't believe me, then I'll say it as many times as you need to hear it. *I love her.* You don't know what I would give to convince you how genuinely sorry I am for hurting your mother. And I promise you with everything inside of me, I am not going to hurt Juliet like that, and I'm not going to break her heart. You already did one bold, crazy thing today that you thought you'd never do. Can't you be daring enough to do one more? Please, Vienna, I'm asking you to just trust me."

CHAPTER NINE

"I'm sorry, Mom. I'm sorry I kissed Maxi."

A sobbing Vienna repeated the words over and over as she knelt on the cemetery grounds in front of her mother's grave. She hadn't cried very much in her life, and the feeling of it still seemed weird to her. She hung her head down, wanting to sink into the ground herself and join her mother.

"I don't know what I was thinking. I hate him for what he did to you, and I hate myself for letting him do what he did to me. I hate myself for taking pleasure in it."

She touched the grey stone slab as a cool breeze blew by, caressing the blades of grass all around her while it began to dry her tears. It almost felt like her mother's way of forgiving her.

But that wasn't a good enough sign for Vienna.

"I criticized Jules for sleeping with him, and then look at what I did. Damn him! He got to both of us. I promise I'll never kiss him again. And please, forgive Jules. She doesn't know what she's doing. He got into her blood like a virus, and God damn it, she can't shake him. She's too weak. If Dad were here, none of this would be happening." She studied the grave for a long time before shaking her head hopelessly. "How could you do it, Mom? There's got to be *something* worth living for."

"You kissed my father?"

Vienna whirled around to find Cassandra standing a few feet

behind her, near a weeping willow tree. "Geez, Cass, you scared the hell out of me!"

"Why did you kiss my father?"

Vienna was shocked by Cassandra's vexed tone. The fire-engine red shade of Cassandra's cotton top and mini-skirt matched the angry flush in her cheeks. What happened to the jolly girl who never let anything bother her? Vienna feared that her own hostile behavior was starting to rub off on her best friend. Cassandra was in serious need of a new role model. A perplexed Vienna scrambled to her feet and dusted off a few blades of grass from her legs, wondering how to deal with this unexpected turn of events.

And yet with the colorful jumble of thoughts that were tumbling around in her brain, she somehow managed to make a trivial observation about how appropriate it was that a "weeping" willow tree was situated right in the middle of a cemetery, amongst mourners.

Today, though, Vienna was the only mourner there. The cemetery, like Clover Lane and practically every other street in Tiger Lily, was dead, too. Something odd, even sinister, was going on. It had been going on for the past three weeks. Kids weren't riding their bikes anymore or playing outside. Mothers weren't taking walks with their babies in strollers. Joggers were nowhere in sight. Where was the perpetually cheerful Dr. Thorne, with his signature fluorescent green headband and matching wristbands? And why wasn't sweet little Charlotte Sloane outside in her beautiful garden reading the latest murder mystery with Butterscotch by her side, rubbing her orange-ringed tail against Charlotte's legs? Vienna was beginning to wish she were back at the dorm at Columbia, amidst the hustle and bustle of New York's streets. Sure, the dorm itself might be dead right now because of summer vacation, but at least outside she would be among the land of the living.

For now, though, she had more pressing problems at hand.

"What are you doing here, Cass?" Vienna asked. "What time is it?"

"Five-thirty."

"My God, is it that late already?" Vienna exclaimed.

"What time did you get here?"

Vienna shrugged. "I don't know. Around four-thirty, I guess."

"You've been at your mom's grave for a whole hour?"

Vienna scratched her head. "Have I? Funny, it doesn't feel that long."

"Are you okay?"

"I'm fine," Vienna said.

"How did you make out at your interviews?"

"They went well," Vienna said. "But I won't know anything until next week."

"I called your house because I was worried about you. I wanted to see how you were doing after what happened with my dad and Jule last night. I got your answering machine, but I know you've been coming here a lot, so I took a chance that I might find you here."

"You didn't tell Jules you were coming here, did you?" Vienna asked.

"No. But I spoke to my dad, and he's worried about you."

"Oh, God!" Vienna breathed. A sinking feeling of death shot through her body just from the mention of Maxi. She had to take a moment to catch her breath. "Cass, I was sharing a very private moment with my mother just now, and I would appreciate it very much if you would let me get back to it. And please, don't tell anyone you saw me here. Not my sister and especially not your father. I can't deal with anyone right now."

"Why did you kiss my father?"

"I don't know," Vienna said.

"Have you been lying to me all these years that you've been saying you hate him?"

"No, I really *do* hate him! I think he's an arrogant, narcissistic wiseass who thinks every woman in the world is supposed to find him irresistible."

"Apparently you're one of those women."

"He came on to me, Cass."

"Why would he do that? He likes Juliet, not you."

"I'm telling you, Cass, he was relentless!"

"So why didn't you stop him?"

"I tried to," Vienna said, "but he kept coming after me. After a while I started to enjoy it."

A heavier breeze blew Cassandra's dark hair into her face. She angrily pushed it aside. The rabid look in her hazel-green eyes was five times more tempestuous than any look that Vienna had ever given Maxi.

"Come on, Cass, don't look at me like that. What the hell, I'm only flesh and blood. I'm sorry, okay? I don't know what else to say."

Vienna looked blankly up at the sky, wishing she could pull a better explanation out of the air. The blue sky was turning misty grey and ominous, like the lifelessness of Tiger Lily during the past three weeks. Monstrous charcoal-grey clouds were hovering above her, which was extremely creepy, considering that the skies were always clear and sunny in Tiger Lily. Vienna wondered whether this was Mother Nature's way of telling her, "You're screwed." Yep, she was a dead woman all right, and she was in the right place for it, too. She peered down at the shiny yellow buttercups around her mother's grave. They gave her a little comfort right now, because they were the only happy things in sight. Maybe her mother was trying to tell her that she forgave her for kissing Maxi.

"How could you do this to me?" Cassandra said with agony in her voice, shaking her head like she'd never felt so disappointed and offended in her life. "How could you do this to *me*? For five years I've known you, I've been loyal to you and stuck by you through thick and thin, and you have the gall to do this to me?"

"I didn't do anything to you! I did it to my mother. That's why I'm here."

"Now you listen to me, Vienna," Cassandra said, sticking out her index finger. "I'm not thrilled that my father is sleeping with Juliet, but I can tolerate it. I know those two have been drawn to each other for a very long time. You and my dad, however . . ." She wagged her head. "That just doesn't make any sense. Although maybe it does, when I think about it. You're both very passionate, strong-willed people. You're really a better match for him than Juliet is. You're fiery and feisty, and—"

"I don't want to hear anymore of this, Cass. I have no interest in your father, and I'm very sorry that I kissed him."

"Were both of you drunk?" Cassandra asked.

"No!"

"Did you kiss him in the hopes that Juliet would walk in and catch you two, and she'd think my dad was cheating on her and she'd dump him?"

Vienna pondered this for a second. "Damn, I wish *I'd* thought of that!" She laughed. "Cass girl, there's a sneaky side to you that nobody ever sees. You're a closet bad girl."

"Oh, please tell me you're not actually going to do that."

"No, I couldn't do that to my own sister," Vienna said. "Besides, it probably wouldn't work."

"So you're not going to kiss him again?"

"No, of course not," Vienna said.

"Because if you do, things will never be the same between you and me."

Something strange was going on, and Vienna wasn't in the right frame of mind to deal with it after her embarrassing ordeal with Maxi, not to mention the two nerve-wracking job interviews.

"How far did it go with him, Vienna? Did you have sex with him?"

"No! What the hell's going on, Cass? You said you didn't have an Electra complex. What is this weird, psychosexual connection between fathers and daughters? You don't need to be jealous of me."

"I'm not jealous of you. You don't get it, do you? I told you this morning, but you didn't hear me. Or you heard me, but you didn't listen."

"Told me what?" Vienna asked.

Tears were welling up in Cassandra's eyes. "I love you!"

"I know that, Cass. I love you, too. You're my best friend."

Cassandra sighed and closed her eyes. She sobbed endlessly, her shoulders shaking. Suddenly Vienna realized how stupid and insensitive she'd been, not thinking about what she said before she'd said it. For five years, she'd assumed that all she'd been to Cassandra was a friend. She'd assumed that Cassandra liked guys. But now that Vienna thought about it, she couldn't remember the last time she saw Cassandra flirt with a guy. She didn't remember Cassandra *ever* flirting with a guy. The more Vienna thought about it, the more it made sense. In all those years, Cassandra never once talked about a guy she liked or a Hollywood heartthrob. She never went on dates even though guys asked her out all the time.

Vienna looked at Cassandra for what felt like an eternity, wishing she hadn't gotten so annoyed by her relentless questions. She had to smooth things over now, somehow, without appearing uneasy after this sudden revelation.

"I'm sorry, Cass. I didn't know. Why didn't you tell me?"

"Because you've always had other things on your mind, eating away at you." She wiped her tears. "I'm sorry. I shouldn't have torn into you like that."

"Forget about it." Vienna embraced her. "I know we've all been on edge lately. And now we've both lost our moms. Now is really the time for us to stick together, more than ever before. I should try to remember that."

Cassandra responded wholeheartedly to Vienna's embrace, holding her close and burying her face in Vienna's shoulder. It was at that moment that Vienna felt the depth of Cassandra's affection for her.

"I guess I never knew you liked guys," Cassandra said.

"Neither did I. Or maybe I just forgot I did, and your dad reminded me."

When they drew apart, Cassandra made an effort to smile.

"I'm glad that he helped you," she said. "Glad he finally did something nice for you."

"Yeah, I guess that's one way to look at it. Who would have thought?" Vienna paused a moment. "I'm sorry, Cass. I don't think my heart has enough of whatever it takes to love anyone right now, man or woman."

Cassandra looked at her tenderly for a moment. She moved closer to Vienna, bringing her lips near hers like she was toying with the idea of kissing Vienna on the mouth. Then she moved her mouth to the left and upward. She kissed Vienna genuinely on the cheek.

"Don't always put yourself down," she said softly.

Vienna smiled. "I'll walk home with you."

"No, I think you should stay here. Do what you have to do. I should visit my mom's grave, too."

Vienna wasn't planning to stay there, but she did know what she had to do.

CHAPTER TEN

"Just this morning, Romy, Cassandra was encouraging me to go out and find someone to love. I thought she meant a man. I didn't know she meant her."

"Is she okay?"

Vienna felt a little weary. It had been one hell of a day, and right now Romy's cozy living room sofa was a nice refuge from the rest of the world—even from the people she loved. Just observing the activity in the aquarium on Romy's bay window put Vienna at ease and relaxed her. The bright red, blue, and green Siamese fighting fish brushed past the greenery with their flowing fins, swimming to the surface occasionally with puckered lips as they checked for leftover granules of food. Some of the pebbles at the bottom of the tank even matched the colors of the fish. Romy had always been good at color coordination. Even the royal blue carpet and blue sofa matched with the pebbles and the fish. And even Romy's cobalt blue blouse and pants set matched with them. Vienna supposed all that blueness made sense, since Romy lost her best friend three weeks ago.

Vienna looked beyond the fish tank at the backdrop of furry pussy willows outside the bay window, the wispy garnet-hued mimosa, and the glossy yellow buttercups on Romy's front lawn. Seeing those sunny buttercups again reminded Vienna of her mother. From a distance, the white flowers on the azalea bushes looked like shredded coconut flakes, and the mimosa resembled massive sprays of feathers dipped in burgundy wine. All that plant life relaxed Vienna even more. Even the word "mimosa" had a soothing ring to it.

"Vienna?"

"Hm? Oh, I'm sorry, Romy. Guess I'm a little distracted."

"Are you and Cassandra okay?"

"Oh, yeah, we're still friends."

Romy put her arm around Vienna. "Something else is bothering you. What is it?"

"Nothing either of us can do anything about."

Romy nodded. "I see. Maxi and Juliet slept together last night."

"How did you know?"

"What else could it be?" Romy patted her arm warmly. "He won't hurt her. In his eyes, she's a fragile and delicate creature, and hurting her would be like mutilating a swan."

"I wasn't home at the time. I spent the night at Cassandra's. We were up late watching movies. Come to think of it, she did find it odd that Maxi never called to say he wasn't coming home. In any case, I walked home this morning with Cassandra. She wanted to pay Jules a visit. Jules came bouncing down the stairs high as a kite, hugging me and Cassandra. Her face was glowing. She couldn't stand still, she was so excited. I thought she was on speed."

"I wish I'd seen her," Romy said. "I don't think I've ever seen Jule that happy before."

"He's the last person she should be with."

"I think he sees something in her that's becoming rarer in this world with every passing day," Romy said.

"What's that?"

"Sweetness. Innocence. Does that mean he loves her?" Romy shrugged. "Who are we to say? She's not a minor, so technically they have a right to do whatever they want to do."

Vienna was surprised at Romy's nonchalant attitude, considering that Romy was a strict Catholic who attended mass every Sunday and took part in the weekly readings from time to time. She also headed the committee that put together the annual craft fair, an activity whose purpose was to raise money for the church's maintenance needs. Every year during the Lenten season, Romy joined a faith-sharing group. At Christmas time, she helped to wrap and distribute gifts for poor children. She was always donating bags of food and bundles of clothing to disadvantaged people, and she occasionally went on soul-searching retreats with other members of her parish. Wooden crucifixes hung on her walls, and statues of the Blessed Mother with the Christ child were scattered throughout her house.

And yet Romy was acting indifferent about Juliet's night of premarital passion with Maxi. Vienna was more than a little puzzled.

"This sounds weird coming from you, Romy."

"Juliet knows I feel the same way you do about this. I just have a quiet way of showing it. Jule herself is usually pretty quiet and a little shy, but don't let that fool you. She's a very determined young woman, and when she wants something, she doesn't let go of it."

Vienna nodded. "Tell me about it."

She could feel Romy studying her face as she peered listlessly at the mahogany coffee table.

"So tell me, what else is bothering you?" Romy asked.

Vienna looked up. "That's right, I haven't gotten to that yet, have I?"

"Take your time. By the way, how did your interviews go?"

"Pretty well, but I won't hear any news for another week."

"How are your night classes going, Vien?"

"Great. The computer class is advanced, and the women who interviewed me seemed impressed by that, and they both liked that I'm a business major."

"Which class do you have tonight?" Romy asked.

"Neither. I'm off on Friday." Vienna leaned toward Romy in shame. "I did something horrible, Romy. You're not going to believe this. I kissed Maxi."

Romy scrunched up her eyebrows. "You did what?"

"He's got some dumb-ass idea swirling around in his brain that I've been putting on a big front all these years, acting like I hate him when I'm really in love with him."

"Are you?"

"No! Romy, you know I hate that man more than the devil. In my mind, he *is* the devil."

"And still you kissed him?"

"He said I don't know how to act like a woman," Vienna said. "So he tested me. He came on to me! And I fell for it and kissed him back. I don't know why." She studied the spiral design of the professionally sculpted bushes and shrubs on Romy's front lawn, and she thought about how twisted her own life was becoming. "I felt so guilty about it that I ran to my mom's grave and apologized left and right to her for kissing the man who used to hit her. It was like what you do in confession, Romy. I needed to come clean."

"Oh, Vienna, you kissed a man, that's all. You haven't betrayed your mother by kissing Maxi. What he did was out of line, but it was clever in a way. He wanted to see another side to you, a side you never show anyone—not even yourself. You should be grateful to him. He's bringing you in touch with your sexuality."

Vienna nodded. "That's what Cassandra said—that he helped me."

"And underneath all of your guilt, you feel good about that, don't you?"

"I don't know," Vienna said. "Maybe."

"And that makes you feel even guiltier. And maybe what makes you feel even guiltier is that you want to kiss him again, maybe even sleep with him. Or maybe you already slept with him, and that's the *real* reason why you feel so guilty."

Vienna laughed. "Romy, you're really doing a bang-up job playing shrink, but I think you're getting a little carried away with it. You know I would never sleep with that man."

"Well, I think you should feel good about the kiss. This is a turning point for you. Think of it this way: you were extending an olive branch to him."

Vienna laughed. "Yeah, right!"

"Your mother forgave him."

"Maybe, but I can't," Vienna said. "And I can't forget about her suicide note."

"I think you're making too much of that."

"Romy, she killed herself because of whatever she was referring to in that letter." Vienna sat forward on the sofa and folded her hands together calmly. "Romy, tell me, is there something about my mother's past that you don't want me and Jules to know about? Something dark and sinister? Because either way it's a no-win situation. I'm damned if I know and damned if I don't know. So if you do know something, I'd rather you just tell me and be done with it."

"Vienna, believe me, your mother was not raped. If she were, she would have told me. She never would have kept quiet about that."

"But let's say she did keep quiet for some reason."

"What reason could that be?" Romy asked.

Vienna shrugged. "Maybe she killed the guy in self-defense, and she was afraid to go to the cops because she didn't think they'd believe her."

"No, I can't imagine that being the case."

"Romy, she said she felt ashamed, angry, and violated. Something awful happened to her, I can feel it. Something of a criminal nature. And I can't go to the cops, because I have no evidence. All I have is a letter saying that some man—we don't know who—did something to her—we don't know what. He violated her, but we don't know how!"

"Vienna, I think you're blowing things way out of proportion. If you reread the letter, you'll notice that it says he violated her *trust*—not her. There are plenty of non-violent ways a man can violate a woman's trust without violating the woman herself. He can lie to her or cheat on her."

"She said she was ashamed of what people were going to say about her behind her back if they knew. Knew what? For all we know, maybe he got her pregnant. Maybe she got an abortion, and then she felt guilty and ashamed afterward. Who knows?"

"Vienna, I don't think you should make wild speculations about your mother. It's no way to honor her memory."

"I only want to know the truth."

"What you want is to kill Maxi," Romy said. "Isn't that right?"

"Yes, I do. And if I find out that he raped my mother, I'm damn well *gonna* kill him!"

"I don't want to hear you talk like that, Vienna."

"I have this nagging feeling that something catastrophic is going to happen, to all of us. Something that we won't be able to bounce back from, and it's going to be because of Maxi. It's like death. You know it's coming but you don't know the exact date, and you don't know what form it will take. That's what this premonition feels like. I can't shake it, Romy. Maybe that's why this town has been so dead these past few weeks. Everyone is picking up the same dreadful vibes as I am, and they don't want to be anywhere in sight when disaster strikes."

Romy had her hand on her chin, apparently thinking about this. "You know, now that you mention it, it *has* been like a ghost town around here lately."

Vienna nodded. "Ever since my mom died." She thought about how Tiger Lily's lifelessness mimicked the emptiness she'd been feeling ever since her mother's suicide. She peered outside the bay window, hoping to see a bird or some other sign of life on Romy's front lawn or in the dogwood tree, but there was nothing. "When I went away to college I was actually happy for a while, after everything he did to her. I was actually living a normal life, until I found out that Mom blew her brains out. Then I came back here, and suddenly we're all right back where we started—with Maxi! Everything is always about Maxi. God damn sun's gonna stop shining the day they shovel dirt on him." Her head suddenly became achy, and her tired eyes became absently transfixed on the coffee table as she heard herself quietly murmur, "There has to be something worth living for, besides revenge."

Romy gently squeezed her hand. "Whatever it is, I'll help you find it, Vienna. I promise you."

"Thanks, Romy. Say, do you mind if I crash here tonight? I feel like getting away from everybody."

"No problem. I'm interviewing a few people in the morning, so I'd like to get to the office a little early to review their resumes. So if I'm not here when you wake up, that's where I'll be."

Vienna nodded. "Okay, I'll lock up. Thanks, Romy. You're an angel." She furrowed her brows in confusion. "Wait a minute. Tomorrow's Saturday. You're conducting interviews?"

"We don't normally do that at Pinkerton, but we need to fill these positions as soon as possible. They've been posted for over a month. We wanted to hire people within the company, but unfortunately no in-house people responded. So we had to go with outside candidates."

"Any jobs I might be interested in?" Vienna asked.

"Sorry, Vien. No summer jobs. There's an opening for a customer service rep, a cash manager in the mutual fund accounting department, and a front desk receptionist."

"Maybe when I graduate I'll apply, if there are any openings."

"Pinkerton always has openings," Romy said. "You could start out as a commissions clerk or cash manager's assistant. Remember, you have experience working there, those summers when you helped out me and your mom with those data entry projects."

"That's true. I mentioned that in my resume."

"You can do anything you want to do," Romy said. "You've been carrying a 4.0 grade point average every semester for the past three years at an Ivy League school! Do you have any idea how phenomenal that is?"

"Cassandra mentioned that, too. I have Maxi to thank for that. I think all these years I've been channeling my hatred for him into my school work. My anger has been making my blood flow a little more strongly, and it's given me more brain power."

Romy smiled softly. "So he's helped you in two ways. He's putting you in touch with your sexuality, and he's helping you with your education."

"Yeah, whatever." Vienna touched Romy's arm. "Thank you for helping my mom take care of me and Jules." She smiled. "And for putting up with my crap, when I socked Maxi at Mom's funeral. And when I punched out Kelly Kline and Richard. I know my mom bent your ear about that." She did her best to imitate Felicity. "'That girl of mine is a wild animal! I don't know where she got that temper. What in hell am I going to do about her? Why can't she be like her sister? Jule is such an angel, so sweet and lily-white. Sometimes I think this town was named after my two girls. Vienna is a tiger and Juliet is a lily.'"

Romy smiled. "Yeah, that was Felicity all right."

"I love you, Romy. I want to tell you that now, because I may not get the chance later."

"Why not? What's going to happen?"

Vienna shrugged. "I'm afraid to find out."

CHAPTER ELEVEN

At the boutique that afternoon, Juliet received a dozen roses from Maxi. The card simply read, "To my precious 'jewel,' Love, Maxi." She blushed when she saw that the roses were pink. It reminded her of the beautiful, manly way that he'd kissed and sucked on her pink nipples last night. She was amazed that she'd felt so refreshed all through the day, in spite of the fact that she'd spent the night making love with Maxi and hadn't gotten much sleep. The scrawny blond delivery boy kept staring at her and smiling, looking her over from head to toe like he wanted to ask her out himself and was jealous of this mysterious Maxi. Or maybe he noticed the sexy glow in her cheeks and the faraway smile, and he figured out what kind of night she'd had. As he was leaving, he glanced over his shoulder at her one last time and winked. The silver bell over the doorway tinkled cheerfully, as though echoing his good-natured personality. Juliet found a glass vase in the back room and set the roses on the counter by the cash register. She was pleased that they added an extra splash of spring color to the boutique's atmosphere.

Around six o'clock Miranda Key, the stunning blond from yesterday, came into the store and browsed at the satin evening bags on the wooden shelves again. Her violet-blue Liz Taylor eyes sparkled as she smiled at Juliet. She was quite a sight, with a shapely and statuesque figure that was guaranteed to turn the heads of men everywhere, and Juliet could tell that Miranda knew it. It was in the way that she rocked her hips from side to side when she walked, like she had the art of feminine motion down to a science. Her fluffy, platinum blond hair revealed dark roots, making Juliet wonder what Miranda once looked like in her natural brunette tresses. Miranda wore a generous amount of make-up, but she carried it off well because of her chiseled facial features. Juliet also noticed that Miranda wore the same kinds of business suits that Vienna wore, with a blazer and a short matching skirt. Today she was wearing a bright red suit with matching leather pumps as she clutched a red eelskin purse. Her long red nails glistened as she swept her hand over the lace and satin camisoles and nightgowns that were hanging on a circular rack in the center of the boutique with a "Fifty Percent Off" sign on top. She selected a long, sea foam green satin nightgown with spaghetti straps and a matching robe.

"I love this shop," she said when she was ready to make her purchase. "I didn't get a chance to see everything yesterday. I had to be somewhere."

"It's just as well," Juliet said. "I had to close up shortly after you left anyway, since we close at six on Thursdays. But today we're open till eight." She carefully folded the lingerie and placed it in the box. "You're lucky you came back today. It's the last day of the sale. But we'll be having another one in a couple more weeks, on the wallets and accessories right here." She pointed to the glass display case by the cash register, strategically aiming her index finger at a red eelskin wallet that matched Miranda's purse.

But Miranda seemed to be distracted by the roses. "Wow, those flowers are beautiful!" she said as she pulled some bills and change out of her wallet and handed the money to Juliet.

Juliet smiled proudly. "Thanks. My boyfriend sent them to me." She put the box in a lavender bag and stuffed lavender tissue inside.

"He obviously adores you," Miranda remarked.

"Maxi is a wonderful man, for sure."

Suddenly a shadow hung over Miranda's face, and her body stiffened a little. Her thin, brown penciled eyebrows were pushed together drastically.

"Maxi?" she said softly, almost fearfully.

"His full name is Maximilian."

Miranda grabbed the bag and hustled toward the door without saying another word.

"Are you okay?" Juliet asked.

Miranda ignored her and rushed out the door, her red high heels clacking against the pavement outside.

CHAPTER TWELVE

Juliet found Miranda's address in the telephone directory and headed to her place as soon as she'd closed the boutique. Miranda lived in a two-story, garden style apartment complex. A mallard duck was paddling around in the pond out front, her four fuzzy ducklings trailing close behind in a zig-zag. That was one of the only signs of animal life that Juliet had seen in Tiger Lily in weeks. Pink tulips and dogwood trees with snow-white flowers brightened the freshly mowed lawn. Miranda's first-floor apartment was across from the pond.

"Do you know my boyfriend?" Juliet asked as soon as Miranda opened the door.

Miranda looked annoyed by the disturbance but answered her anyway.

"I think I do."

But just as she opened her mouth to say more, Juliet stopped her.

"Wait. Whoever it is that Maxi reminds you of, tell me what his last name is. I want to make sure we're talking about the same man."

"His last name is Ward."

Juliet hesitated for a few seconds before going on. "How do you know him?"

Miranda's eyes looked a little sinister now. "You sure you want to know?"

"Yes."

Miranda crinkled her forehead. "I don't think you do."

"Oh, I do," Juliet said firmly.

Miranda invited her inside. Everything in the apartment was bright red—the shag carpet, the telephone on the wall, and the leather sofa and chairs. The coffee table was red glass with a brass rim. The red walls were covered with paintings of red cardinals in flight, red apples and strawberries in a red ceramic bowl, and the red sands of the Kalahari Desert. Every painting was displayed in a red wooden frame. The mantel was lined with extravagant pieces of red Baccarat crystal. In the center of the round, red glass dining room table sat a red glass vase that was filled with red tulips.

As Juliet passed by the bathroom, she noticed that the toilet, towels, shower curtain, sink, counter, toothbrush, toothbrush holder, wastebasket, and liquid soap dispenser were all red. Feeling like Sissy Spacek in *Carrie*, Juliet stood dead still in the middle of the living room and rubbed her eyes. She just knew she had to be seeing things.

"You okay?" Miranda asked.

Juliet tried to smile. "I'm fine, thanks."

Miranda pulled a pack of cigarettes out of her red purse. "You want a smoke?"

Juliet politely declined. Miranda lit a cigarette with her red plastic lighter and took a long drag. "Maxi and I went to Tiger Lily High together. He was two grades ahead of me. One weekend in my sophomore year, we ran into each other at a party at someone's house, and we started talking. He had the most incredible eyes, like none I'd ever seen before or since. He'd been drinking a little too much, but we were having a lot of fun talking, laughing, and dancing. Maxi was pretty slick with the girls back then. The Romeo of Tiger Lily High, you know what I mean? He's got that sexy beauty mark near his eye and those cute dimples no girl can resist. Seemed like every time I passed him in the hall, he was kissing someone. Oh, he was one hot number back in school, let me tell you. He burned up the stage when he starred in 'Bye Bye Birdie.' Swiveled those hips like Elvis come back from the dead. The girls went wild. I can still hear the screams."

"The high school heartthrob, hm? I heard he was a little shy back then."

"He was shy in class," Miranda said, "but in social situations he was a real wild man. Every girl I knew had it bad for him. The only woman he couldn't charm was the principal. She ran into more problems with Maxi than with any other kid in school. All of it involving girls, too. Getting into fights in the hallway over a girl, doing speed in the quad with a girl—"

"Speed? Really?" Juliet said, trying to appear astonished but in truth suspending belief until she'd heard Maxi's side of the story.

"A gym teacher even caught him having sex with the homecoming queen in the girls' locker room after the class let out and the other girls had left. Can you believe it?"

"Get out!"

Miranda nodded. "In the shower. The teacher heard moans and cries coming from the showers, and she thought someone was hurt. Big surprise when she saw them, huh? Come to think of it, I think he got caught a couple of times having sex in school. I forget where the other place was."

She puffed on her cigarette as she circled the living room quietly, apparently trying to remember the location of the other place. Juliet prayed she wouldn't. Listening to Miranda talk about Maxi's sexual conquests in high school wasn't her idea of fun. She tried not to let Miranda see how much it angered her, but the color of her emotion was definitely a shade of red that was even brighter than the lipstick red that saturated Miranda's apartment.

"I think it was in a classroom, on the teacher's desk," Miranda recalled. "The teacher was coming back from lunch, and he found them there." She took another drag on her cigarette. "Wasn't the homecoming queen that time. I think the girl was a freshman." She looked at Juliet and kinked up her eyebrow. "Wild stuff, huh?"

"You're telling me. Sex, drugs, fights—anything else?" Juliet asked, suddenly feeling like a homicide detective conducting an investigation.

"At school?" Miranda shrugged. "Nothing else I can remember offhand."

"What about this party you started to tell me about?"

Miranda's face turned grim and pale. She clutched her forehead as though struggling to recall the night's events.

"Do you remember what happened that night, Miranda?"

"Maxi and I started to slow dance, but the house got so crowded that we barely had room, so we went outside and got in his car. We didn't drive anywhere. I wouldn't have let him anyway, because he was drunk. We just sat in the car and kissed for a while. Maxi was legendary at Tiger Lily High for being a great kisser. For a while I was having a good time. He was even better than I thought he'd be. But then his hand started to creep up my skirt. I told him to stop, but he wouldn't listen. I kept screaming at him to stop, but he got forceful, and before I knew it—" Her lips trembled. Tears ran down her cheeks. "He raped me! He covered my mouth while he did it, so no one could hear me scream. But no one would have heard me anyway. Everyone at the party was in the house, and the music was blasting. I could hear it from outside." She sobbed uncontrollably. "No one could help me. I pressed charges against him and took him to court, but the jury found him innocent."

Suddenly Juliet felt sick inside. After the colorful tales Miranda had told five minutes ago, Juliet had him pegged as nothing more than a macho teenager whose adolescent hormones picked the wrong time to go into overdrive. But now she looked at Miranda and swallowed hard as she realized the gravity of the situation.

"The jury didn't have enough evidence to convict him?" Juliet asked.

Miranda paced the floor as she wiped her tears. "The defense attorney questioned me about my sexual history." She took another drag from her cigarette. "My high school days were pretty wild ones. I slept around with guys I barely knew. But that night I told Maxi no. When he got on the witness stand, he said he couldn't remember hearing me say no because he was drunk. That's why the jury let him go."

She sat on the couch and sobbed, her face buried in her hands. The familiar cries of despair haunted Juliet. She'd heard them at her mother's funeral. They were her own cries.

"It took years before I could finally put this behind me," Miranda said. "I spent hours in a shrink's office, during my entire junior year of high school." Her body trembled. "I couldn't go on a date without cringing in fear whenever the guy tried to kiss me or even hold my hand. Even if I was just walking down the street and a guy looked at me for more than a second, my stomach got choked up with nausea. For years I thought I'd never be able to get married, because I'd be too traumatized to sleep with a man." Her hand shook as she crushed out her cigarette in the red glass ashtray atop the coffee table. "When

I reached my twenties, I started to feel a little less afraid. I went out with men I met at the accounting firm where I used to work." She pulled a pack of tissues out of her purse and blew her nose. "It's still hard for me, but I'm getting by. But I figured he moved away a long time ago. I didn't know he still lived in Tiger Lily!" She burst into tears again. "Oh, God, why can't he just move away?"

Juliet sighed. "I'm sorry for what you went through. Truly sorry."

"I know you don't want to believe me. I realize this is hard for you, but I swear it's true. Please don't tell him where I live. I don't want him coming after me."

Juliet nodded solemnly. "I understand."

Miranda's teary face was twisted with contempt and torment. Her eyes seared with fire. "Part of me hasn't been the same since he raped me, and I don't think I ever will be. You seem like a nice girl, Juliet. Please, do yourself a favor. Stay away from him."

CHAPTER THIRTEEN

It was no coincidence that Miranda Key had come into Delilah's Boutique to buy a nightgown. It was no coincidence that she came on the very same day that Maxi had sent Juliet roses. It wasn't even a coincidence that her last name was Key. She held the "key" to solving the mystery of Felicity's rape. This had to be a sign, the kind of clue that Vienna had been dying to find. She'd been right from the very beginning. Maxi was Felicity's rapist.

Juliet left Miranda's around nine and sped out of the parking lot in her white Nissan, heading straight for Maxi's house ten blocks away. Unfortunately she hit all the red lights. Her breath came heavy as she whacked the steering wheel impatiently and watched some jerk in the left lane go through the red light. Damn you, Maxi Ward! If Vienna knew about this . . . well, Juliet wasn't going to think about that right now. She hated the thought of more people dying, and that was exactly what Vienna had in store for Maxi.

Green light! Juliet whizzed past Tiger Lily Mall and the sparse amount of cars that were scattered throughout the parking lot. She passed the red brick high school, then Stefano's a few blocks further down. That was the intimate little Italian restaurant she'd always dreamt of going to with Maxi. Now it seemed like that dream was shot to hell. She drove past the office complex with the grey-tinted windows where Romy worked. Three more blocks. Juliet made a sharp right and spun around the corner, slowing down as she approached the stop sign at the next block. The closer she got to Maxi's house, the stronger her heart pounded.

Maxi greeted her at the door with a smile and a lilt in his voice. "There's my beautiful girl!"

He closed the front door and held her close, moistening her with kisses on her lips and cheeks. She had planned on tearing into him immediately, but now that he was bathing her in the sensual warmth of his body heat, she remained frozen in his arms. She closed her eyes, wanting to squirm out of his grasp but unable to find the strength. His crisp white shirt felt so good against her cheek, and the heady scent of his musk cologne was working its magic on her.

"God, you smell sensational," he whispered. "Which scent is this one?"

"Vanilla. Thank you for the roses, Maxi. They've really dressed up the boutique."

"I'm glad you like them." He kissed her. "I couldn't wait to see you, baby girl."

She couldn't understand why he was being so amorous with her before she even took five steps into the house. She was almost afraid he was going to strip off her clothes right then and there and make love to her. And what's worse, she was afraid she would let him, in spite of the big question mark in her mind about Miranda Key. She had to free herself from his embrace, and fast, because she realized now that she was playing with fire—and enjoying it.

He looked at her sore lips and the love bites on her neck. "Did I hurt you last night?"

"No, not in a bad way."

"Your customers probably thought you were attacked." He leaned in close to her. "I get a little carried away sometimes during sex," he whispered almost shamefully, as though he were sitting in the dark confines of a confessional.

"I think we both did, Maxi."

"So how do you feel today, baby girl? It's the day after your first time. You feel okay?"

"I feel fine," she said, "even though we didn't get much sleep."

He looked into her eyes. She could tell that he knew something was wrong.

"I did hurt you, didn't I?" he said.

"No! If you did, Maxi, I would have told you last night. And I wouldn't have spent the whole night making love to you."

"That isn't what I mean. Listen, Jule, I said some things last night that I shouldn't have said. And there were things that I *should* have said that I didn't say."

"It doesn't matter, Maxi."

"Yes, it does. I love you, baby girl. I'm sorry I didn't tell you that last night. And I will never let another man take you out of this town, away from me." His cheeks were slightly flushed, and he laughed a little timidly. "It's been so long since I've told a woman I love her. It feels strange but wonderful." He kissed her. "You fell in love with me in spite of the horrible way I treated your mother. You believed that I could change." He smiled softly. "You make me want to believe in myself."

She couldn't hear anymore of this. A thousand thoughts rushed through her mind. Maybe Miranda was lying. She had to be. Fate would be too cruel to make him open his heart and say those wonderful things right after Juliet had discovered that he was a rapist. No, he couldn't be. She closed her eyes. In the past twenty-four hours he had warmed, chilled, and then warmed her heart all over again. She had to be realistic. What if he really wasn't the man she had deluded herself into believing he was? What if Miranda had told the truth about him?

"You're wearing my favorite dress, Jule. Why don't we go out tonight, and you can show it off?" He took both her hands in his and leaned his forehead against hers. "Come on, sweetie, don't be angry at me because of the stupid way I acted on our first night together. I want to take my baby girl out tonight and make it up to her."

"I'm sorry, Maxi, I just can't." She pulled her hands out of his grasp.

He eyed her curiously. "You're angry about something else, aren't you? Talk to me, Jule. Tell me what's wrong. You won't kiss me. You won't even smile at me. What did I do?" Just as she opened her mouth, he said, "Wait a minute, I know. Look, I only kissed Vienna because I was testing her."

"You kissed Vienna?"

"Isn't that why you're angry?"

"No, Maxi, it isn't. Why the hell did you do that?"

"She interrogated me because I took you to bed. I started to think that maybe her hostility toward me is masking jealousy and sexual frustration. So I decided to test that theory and see if I could arouse something in her. I came on to her, and what do you know, she responded! And then she walked out of here looking embarrassed and ashamed as hell. I realize now that it was a stupid thing to do, and I'm sorry. I wasn't trying to slight you." He paused a second. "Although I must admit, I did enjoy kissing her. She may be abrasive on the outside, but on the inside she's all woman." He smiled. "Deep down I think we've got a little something going on between us. You know, all those heated arguments. The yelling, the screaming. There's chemistry there. Oh, it's perfectly innocent. Nothing could ever become of it. I love you too much to let that happen, Juliet."

"Mm-hm. Do you call my sister 'baby girl,' too?"

"No, of course not. That's a term of endearment that I reserve only for you, Jule."

"Oh? You never called Miranda Key that?"

He kinked up an eyebrow. "Miranda Key?"

"Yes, Maxi. Does that name ring a bell?"

His face turned chalky white. "I went to high school with her. How do you know her?"

"She bought a nightgown at the boutique today. When she saw the roses you sent me, I mentioned your name." She eyed him with a glacial fierceness. "She says you raped her back in high school."

"That bitch is still lying about that after all these years? I had sex with her, but I certainly didn't rape her."

"Maxi, I just came from her apartment, and she was trembling in fear and sobbing like crazy. She couldn't have been crying because she had a good time." She sighed. "Vienna warned me time and time again. I should have listened to her. Do you know why my mom killed herself, Maxi? She was hurt by some man she knew. It was in her suicide note."

"Hurt how?"

She glared at him. "You tell *me*." She was starting to see fear in his eyes. Rage was building up inside her, more and more with every passing minute. "Did you rape my mother, Maxi?"

"No, of course not!"

She shook her head in disgust. "Everything about you is always such a damn mystery. You won't even tell me why I can't take your Shakespeare class."

"I'm in love with you, Jule! I wouldn't be able to look at your work objectively. I didn't tell you before, because I wasn't ready to talk about my feelings for you."

"Why would Miranda say you raped her if you didn't, Maxi? Was she in love with you? Was she heartbroken because you loved her and left her?"

"No, we both regarded that night as a one-time thing. Look, I have no idea what her problem is, or was. All I know is that she made my life a living hell, dragging me into court for something I didn't do. I never liked that girl. The only reason I had sex with her is because I was tired of being a virgin, and she was the hottest girl in school. And she knew it. She rubbed her hour-glass body up against every guy I knew. That girl was in perpetual heat. You should have seen the clothes she wore to school. Skin-tight sweaters and low-cut, practically see-through tops that were so obviously too small on her. Leather skirts that went all the way up to her ass and exposed her belly button. Even when she was completely covered up, she turned the guys' heads. She may have been a fifteen-year-old, but she sure as hell knew how to walk like a woman—even more so than some of the women I've known. She had sensational body language and a figure that women would kill for.

"But then again, how would I know that? I never got to see it all. That night I had sex with her in my car, she wouldn't take off her black push-up bra. She was on top of me, going at it with me, and she teased me like crazy by pulling the straps off her shoulders and down her arms so that all I saw was the huge upper halves of her breasts bulging out of a bra that was way too skimpy to contain them. Her fingers lingered over the hook in the front of the bra, as though she wanted me to think she was going to take it off, but she didn't. Then she leaned over me so far down that her breasts looked like they were about to spill out of her bra. It's like she was begging me to touch them, and I was dying to. A couple of my friends who had been with her—and *had* seen all of her—told me her breasts were so perfect that she put all the *Playboy* and *Penthouse* centerfolds to shame. I wanted to see for myself.

"So I reached out my hand, but just as my fingers were about to touch her breasts, she swiftly moved away and smiled slyly like she'd gotten away with committing a horrendous crime. I was panting and sweating, not just in lust but in agitation, too. She thought she was so clever, outsmarting me in the bawdy little game she'd invented. You know something? Even the sex wasn't as great as I thought it would be. Actually, it was downright unsatisfying. Maybe she should have done like you do, Jule, and watch some of those racy cable movies to get pointers."

Juliet rolled her eyes. "I think I've heard enough, Maxi."

"Hang in there, sweetie. I'm almost finished. After we had sex, she put her bra straps back on her shoulders and got dressed, laughing haughtily like she was proud of herself because she'd succeeded at working me into a sexual frenzy. As she was getting out of my car, she looked over her shoulder at me and said with a sneer, 'If you were a real man, you'd have had my bra hanging off the rear-view mirror and my nipples in your mouth in no time flat.'" He smiled warmly. "Now that I *am* a real man, I look back on that night, and I realize I was just a stupid kid who made a big mistake. And since then, I've seen and slept with women who are five times more well-endowed than Miranda was back then. I think you already know that you're one of those women, Jule."

"Maxi, I can't help but wonder—"

"Don't worry, baby girl." He fondled her chin. "There haven't been that many other women. Some, but not many."

"It isn't that, Maxi. Something about the scenario you just described doesn't make sense."

"She seduced me, Jule! She tantalized me and played games with me. I bet she did that with a lot of her lovers. She screwed with their minds as well as their bodies. Believe me, she got off on being the vamp of Tiger Lily High."

"Miranda told me you were drunk that night, Maxi."

"Yeah, I was."

"So how can you remember everything so clearly?"

"I don't know, Jule. I just do. When a girl gets a guy stirred up like that, even booze doesn't keep his brain from remembering it. None of my other lovers ever treated me like that." He kissed her cheek. The warmth of his lips spread through her like wildfire. "You're the one person who's always believed in me, who always sees good in me. You know I would never rape anyone. Deep down, you know I never could have raped your mother, because I'm in love with you. Why would I want to hurt you like that?"

His voice was hushed and sexy, like he was making love to her with it. She closed her eyes for just a moment and let her ears relish the sound of it, and she let her senses all through her body take pleasure in the feeling of it. He was always making love to her in one way or another. She let herself take pleasure in the feeling of that, too.

She swallowed hard as powerful feelings of arousal built up within her that she didn't know how to suppress. She realized now that she couldn't escape her love for him. As she closed her eyes, part of her wished that he would disappear from her life for a while and give her a chance to breathe. The other part wanted to get lost inside of him and never come back. She stood there, dead still, waiting and praying for a sign to guide her down the right path. Everything about him pulsated in her blood—and what it did to her just to feel that!

She snuggled into the warmth of his chest, too physically and mentally drained to talk anymore or to fight her feelings for him. He didn't say anything either, as though he understood how she felt and respected her wishes. She liked the silence between them, feeling like it spoke to her and told them they would work through this and come out of it stronger because of it.

"I'm sorry I doubted you," she said.

"Let's just forget about it, Jule." He walked her to the blue leather sofa with his arm around her, and he drew her near as they sat down. "I'm sorry she lied to you. Just try to forget that you ever met her."

"I love you, Maxi." She kissed him.

"I know you do."

They kissed softly for a minute, then the soft kisses gave way to a passionate kiss. Not long after that, they were carrying on like teenagers being attacked by overheated hormones in a parked car, blanketed by the seclusion of the woods. Before she knew it, they were taking off each other's clothes. She whispered over and over how sorry she was while they made love. She felt so stupid and cruel for believing a stranger over him. The more she thought about it, the more passionately she made love to him. Amidst the breathless whirlwind of make up sex, he brushed his hand over the back of her neck and accidentally undid the clasp of her necklace. It slid off her neck and fell on the sofa.

"I'm sorry, Jule." His voice was soft but raspy, and he was panting as though he'd just finished first in a marathon. "We shouldn't be doing this here. Cassandra will be home any minute. She met with the yearbook committee after school, then she went to the mall." He glanced at his watch. "It's ten. The mall is closing." They picked up their strewn clothes from the floor and quickly dressed. "Bad timing, sweetie," he said as he buttoned his white shirt.

She took a moment to catch her own breath while she hooked on her beige satin, strapless bra and pulled on her matching panties. Her whole body felt infused with an inexplicable burst of energy. She never knew that fifteen minutes of fast, hot sex could feel so sinfully exhilarating.

"Let's do something tonight, Maxi, like you wanted to do when I walked in the door."

"Sure, Jule, anything you want to do." He watched her put the necklace back on. "Maybe you should take that off next time, just to be on the safe side."

"No, I've never taken it off. It's very special to me."

"All right, I'll be more careful, I promise." He zipped up her dress.

"Thanks, Maxi." She took both his hands in hers. "I'm sorry Miranda treated you that way. I would never tease you like that."

"I know, baby girl. You satisfy me completely. You never hold anything back from me." He kissed her. "Before we go, maybe we should wait for Cassandra to come home. I really should talk to her about you and me. I don't want her to find out from Vienna."

"She already knows about us, Maxi. I told her this morning."

"How did she take it?"

"She seems fine with it," Juliet said. "But maybe you should talk to her alone. You're her father. She loves you. Maybe she feels uncomfortable, and she doesn't want to tell me."

"Okay, I'll talk to her."

"She needs to know you still love her."

"Of course she knows I love her," he said.

"Tell her, Maxi, all the time. She needs your love even more than I do. She needs you."

He studied Juliet closely. She knew that he knew she was thinking about her own father and what she'd missed out on all her life.

"Come here, baby girl," he whispered, taking her into his arms. "It's okay. Don't feel sad." He stroked her hair and kissed the top of her head. "Sweet girls like you should never feel sad."

She closed her eyes and basked in the remarkable glow of Maxi Ward, and suddenly the sadness inside her evaporated. He had a way with her that no other person on earth could even begin to understand. Sometimes *she* didn't even understand it, but that was all right with her. It was one of the things that made him so mysterious and beautiful.

"Say, Jule, why didn't you tell me about your mom's suicide note before?"

"Because I didn't believe Vienna's suspicions that you raped my mom. Why are you bringing this up now?"

"Because I wish you would have opened up to me and told me, Jule, so I could help you find the man who raped her."

"I think he was someone she trusted. A friend or even someone she loved."

Maxi was silent for a minute, then he said, "Maybe it was your father."

"Excuse me?" She squirmed out of his arms and rose from the sofa. "You didn't even know him, Maxi!"

"You didn't know him either, Jule," he said as he stood up, too.

"But I know that my mom loved him deeply and never said an unkind word about him."

"You said maybe the rapist was a man she loved," he reminded her.

"But I didn't mean my father!"

"As far as you know, Jule, he was the only man she ever loved."

"Oh, you bastard!" She smacked his face, ripped the gold locket off her neck, and flung both the locket and chain in his face. "I can't believe I made love to you again."

"Come on, sweetheart, don't overreact. I was only thinking out loud."

She ignored him and headed out the door, wondering what she ever saw in an insensitive son of a bitch like Maxi Ward.

CHAPTER FOURTEEN

"Jules, why are you sleeping here?" Vienna asked.

"What time is it?" Juliet groggily asked as she sat up on their living room sofa in her icy blue silk nightgown. As she glimpsed at the pattern of red roses in the background of the white sofa, she suddenly felt like she'd been sleeping in a garden.

"It's ten in the morning. What's going on, Jules? Did you sleep here all night?"

"I didn't sleep very much upstairs," Juliet said, pulling her drooping spaghetti strap over her shoulder. "I kept waking up, so I finally decided to come downstairs and have a snack. Then once I got down here, I changed my mind. But since I was already here, I figured I'd just sleep on the sofa."

"Well, whatever."

Juliet stretched her arms. "How did your interviews go?"

"They went well, but the lady who interviewed me has to talk to a few more people. So I won't know for a week." Vienna set her black purse on the wooden table in the vestibule. "I needed some time to myself, so I slept at Romy's."

"Why didn't you call me?"

"I thought you'd be with Maxi," Vienna said.

"Please, don't talk about him."

"Uh-oh, what happened?" Vienna asked as she plopped on the sofa beside Juliet.

"Some woman came into the boutique yesterday and said Maxi raped her."

Vienna's mouth dropped open. "What? Who is this woman?"

"Someone Maxi went to high school with. Miranda Key is her name. She's gorgeous. Looks like Sharon Stone, the way she looked in *Basic Instinct.*"

"So what did she say, Jules?"

"Miranda was a sophomore at the time, and he was a senior. They were at a party one night, dancing and talking. They went outside, and she claims that he raped her. She took him to court. Maxi's lawyer asked her about her sexual past. Turns out she had a wild reputation. Because of that and because he was drunk and said he didn't hear her say no, he got off."

"They had him right there in the courtroom and they let him go?"

Juliet nodded. "But that isn't what bothers me. I was suspicious at first, but not now. This woman is a total stranger. Who knows what her story is?"

"But, Jules, if he did rape her, then it's possible that he raped Mom, too."

"I asked him that point blank. He insisted that he didn't rape anyone. He admits that he had sex with Miranda, but he swears he didn't rape her."

"Hey, where's your locket?" Vienna asked.

"I ripped it off and threw it at him. And I smacked him."

"Wow, Jules, you really *are* pissed off at him! Why? What else happened?"

"In the one short hour that I was at his place, I argued with him, made up with him, made love with him, and then got angry at him all over again and stormed out the door. That man is so unbelievably infuriating!"

Juliet glanced at the pink ceramic, heart-shaped vase on the coffee table. She toyed with the idea of throwing it across the room to vent her frustrations but decided against it, remembering that she wasn't a wild woman like Vienna. Besides, she didn't want to hit the Monet floral print on the wall, not to mention the fact that she had made that vase herself in a pottery class she took in high school.

"Yeah, and you can't wait to have sex with him again, can you, Jules?"

"He said maybe our *dad* raped Mom."

"What the hell!" Vienna cried. "Mom loved Dad. She spent twenty years grieving for him. Maxi knows that. Where the hell does he get off?" She jumped up from the sofa and walked in circles like a gambling addict who'd just lost it all at the casino and didn't know how he was going to go on. "He's making himself look even guiltier of raping Mom by blaming someone else. Someone who loved Mom, no less. But unfortunately, throwing the blame on Dad doesn't prove Maxi is guilty, and Miranda's accusation that he raped *her* doesn't prove it either."

"I think there are pieces to these two puzzles that we haven't found yet. And I think the two incidents are totally unrelated, as far as who committed the crime and whether there even was a crime. I mean, we can speculate all we want to, but we wouldn't get anywhere."

"I asked Romy whether there was something about Mom's past that would shock the hell out of us," Vienna said. "She says there isn't, but I think she'd say or do just about anything to protect us." She sighed. "I hope Maxi's not right about this—that something unspeakably bad went down twenty-one years ago between Mom and Dad. I think you may be right, Jules. There are a lot of weird, sinister things that happened, and someone is keeping us in the dark."

"I know. I hate that." The blood inside of Juliet's head was whirling around ceaselessly like a cat chasing its tail, and her brain felt like it was going to explode. "And you know what's the most pathetic thing about this whole mess? I'm probably going to forgive Maxi for what he said about Dad, and I'll take him back. He always gets his way with me. Even though I'm furious at him, I still know that he's the only man I'll ever love. Something inside me keeps telling me. Something dark and mysterious, like whatever happened to Mom and Miranda. It's like a flashing light. It almost speaks to me."

"Sounds like what I've been feeling lately," Vienna said. "Yesterday I told Romy I love her. I thanked her for everything she's done for us over the years."

Juliet smiled softly. "That's beautiful, Vien."

"But I have this haunting feeling that tells me I need to keep telling her, like I can't say it enough." Vienna looked at the beige carpet pensively. "There's something very telling about this. I just don't know what it is yet." Silence reigned for a minute, then Vienna clapped her hands together with an enthusiasm that Juliet hadn't witnessed in months. "You know what we should do, Jules? Pack our bags and get the hell out of town."

Juliet laughed. "You make it sound like we're running from the law!"

"Well, yeah, we could pretend like we're on some big adventure. Get away from all the melodrama that constantly takes over our lives and just have some fun this weekend."

"Like a couple of regular girls," Juliet said. "I love it! But wait, it's already Saturday. By the time we pack and get to wherever we're going, we'll barely have time down there."

"So we'll just get out of town for the day. We'll hit the road tomorrow morning. We can't do it tonight, since we're spending the evening with Romy."

"Oh, that's right, I forgot she invited us over for dinner," Juliet said. "This will be fun. The Mann sisters hitting the road and raising a little hell. Remember how we always used to say we wanted to go on a little excursion together? When we were fourteen or fifteen?"

Juliet noticed a light in Vienna's silver-blue eyes that she hadn't seen in a very long time, and it warmed her heart to see Vienna look so happy.

"We said as soon as we got our driver's license, we'd go on a road trip," Vienna recalled. "We had no idea where we wanted to go. We were just going to be spontaneous and go wherever the mood took us. Either that or drive down to the Jersey shore, lounge around on the beach, and collect seashells."

"And for some reason we never got around to it."

"Well, this weekend is the weekend, Jules."

"Maybe getting away from here will help me forget about that creepy apartment."

"What apartment?" Vienna asked.

"Miranda's. Everything in it is red. I mean every piece of furniture and every accessory in every room that I saw was fire-engine red, like the woman saw *Carrie* five thousand times and couldn't get the prom scene out of her head."

"Sounds cool!" Vienna said. She headed toward the vestibule and grabbed her purse. "What's her address?"

"Don't go over there, Vien. We really don't know what this woman's story is."

"Ah, who cares? What do you think she's going to do? Murder me?" Vienna laughed. "Maybe that's why everyone on Clover Lane's been staying inside the past few weeks. They're all scared of Miranda Key, psychobitch of Tiger Lily."

"Look, she's obviously furious about *something.* Isn't red the color of anger?"

The doorbell rang. Juliet spotted Maxi's head through the glass on the upper half of the door. She opened the door for him.

"Hi, baby girl."

The second he called her that, she realized how much she'd missed him. He was dressed in black, his best color. His biceps and pectoral muscles were bulging through his form-fitting shirt. The V neckline exposed just enough skin so that a few chest hairs peeked through. Every dark hair on his head was in place, and the lower half of his face was coated with stubble. Never before had she seen him look so sexy. She couldn't believe that she'd had the privilege of making love to this absolutely gorgeous creature. His dark eyes became illuminated when he saw her in a different nightgown.

"You look beautiful, Jule. May I come in?"

"Okay."

He nodded hello to Vienna as he stepped into the vestibule. "I'm sorry I made that insensitive remark about your dad, Jule. I blurted it out without thinking. Please don't be angry at me. You know I would never purposely say anything to hurt you."

The sad little boy was emerging in his tender voice. She could never resist that side of him.

Vienna sulked. "I need to get out of here," she mumbled.

She headed outside and shut the door. Juliet looked at Maxi warmly.

"I'm sorry I smacked you last night, Maxi."

"That's okay. It didn't hurt any." He smiled. "I'm a big, strong man, remember?" He took her hands in his. "So do you forgive me?"

"I always forgive you, don't I?"

He peered at her a little cautiously. "Can I get a good-morning kiss?"

"Go ahead and take it, Maxi." Her voice was daring and playful. "Who's stopping you?"

He reached over and kissed her deeply. As always, the second their lips met, her anger toward him melted away. She tasted the residue of orange juice on the tip of his tongue. That was another part of Maxi's unique allure. He tasted different every time she kissed him. Maybe that was one reason why she loved to lock lips with him more than anything else in the world. With each new kiss, she never knew what to expect.

Afterward, he looked at her with satisfaction in his eyes. "Judging from that kiss, baby girl, I guess you *do* forgive me." He reached into his pants pocket. "I believe you left this at my place."

He pulled out her locket. This time it was suspended from a glistening, diamond-cut gold rope chain that was thicker and much sturdier than the delicate chain it had hung on for the past three years. She studied it closely, watching it glitter brilliantly as she let it cascade over her fingers. The word ITALY was inscribed on the lobster claw clasp, as well as 18K. She could see that this chain was a much richer, more buttery looking kind of gold in comparison with the broken fourteen-karat gold chain.

"Maxi, this chain cost a lot more money. I didn't want you to pay for a new one. I broke the old one, not you."

"It was a pleasure buying you a new one, Juliet."

"I behaved badly yesterday, throwing that at you and—"

He put his index finger on her mouth to quiet her. Without saying a word, he took the necklace out of her hand and draped it around her neck. She swept her hair over one shoulder so that he could clasp the necklace, then he took a step back and glanced at her.

"It looks beautiful," he said.

She looked at herself in the oval beveled mirror in the living room. The light reflected off of the gold rope chain, bringing out the lemon highlights in her blond hair. She touched the locket affectionately. Tears streamed down her face. She gave him a good long embrace, thanking him through muffled sobs and telling him how gorgeous the chain was and how much she loved it.

"After four years, Jule, I thought it was about time I gave my baby girl something."

"Oh, Maxi, I missed you last night."

"I missed you, too."

"I couldn't sleep," she said. "I wanted to be with you, as furious as I was." She kissed him passionately. "I'm sorry I called you a bastard."

"Why? I *am* a bastard sometimes."

"Oh, stop it, Maxi."

"I have something else to show you, Jule."

He took the necklace off her neck, turned the locket over, and lifted it to his lips. She watched him as he closed his eyes and tenderly kissed the back of the locket, his dark and lush eyelashes draped beautifully over his cheeks. Then he handed her the locket, the back side of it still facing upward. On the back of the locket was a script engraving that read:

> "I love you.
>
> Maxi"

She threw her arms around him again. "Thank you, Maxi. I love you, too."

"Why didn't you tell me my picture was in there, Jule? When I asked you about it the other night, you said the locket was empty."

"I guess I wanted you to figure it out for yourself. But what made you open it?"

"After you threw it at me, I figured my picture had to be in there."

She put the locket back on and embraced him again. "This is such a beautiful gesture, Maxi."

"I had more I wanted to put on there, but I ran out of space."

"Tell me, what else?"

He smiled slyly. "Buy another locket, sweetie, and I'll have the rest of the words engraved on *that* one."

She laughed. "Oh, Maxi, you love to keep me wondering, don't you?" She kissed him. "You always make me laugh."

She rubbed her cheek lightly against his bristly face. She kissed him again, needing the warmth of his lips to sustain her. His body heat soaked through her sheer nightgown and penetrated her skin as they kissed. She'd been aching for that heat ever since the moment she saw him standing on her front porch. All the desire she'd felt for him in the past was nothing compared to the feelings that were bubbling up inside her now.

As they parted, he unclasped her necklace and removed it from her neck.

"Maxi—"

"Keep this off, Jule." He stroked the curve of her face. "For now," he whispered.

CHAPTER FIFTEEN

She closed her bedroom door and locked it in case Vienna made an unexpected return appearance. He placed the locket on the nightstand by her bed. They pulled off each other's clothes through a series of mad kisses. The second her nightgown spilled off her body and hit the floor, he sank his lips into her breasts and nipples as though he was escaping into his own world. In the soft and heavenly domain of her magnificent bosom, he seemed to find comfort and solace from the harsh and cruel world of reality. Her nipples were pink, and what did pink symbolize? Innocence? Youth? Maybe he was trying to get out of her those precious gifts that he'd lost so many years ago. And maybe his dark eyes, dark hair, and the beautiful darkness of the night that he loved so much were reflective of the mystery that surrounded him. That mystery was wondrous and entrancing, and she wanted to immerse herself in the sexiness of it. It was enticing and orgasmic, like their love affair. She longed to escape into that unattainable, surrealistic world and lose herself in the very idea that she belonged in it.

"You make me feel so alive," he murmured.

Maybe that was another reason why he loved to suck on her breasts, and moreover, why she loved to kiss him. They wanted to drink in whatever was inside of each other that sent their blood racing and reminded them of their existence on the earth. For whatever reason, they just couldn't get to the heart of it, but they sure had fun trying.

They spent the rest of the morning making love as though they hadn't seen each other in months, doing all the things they'd done before but with more passion and greater stamina. No longer did she feel overwhelmed. She felt freer than ever before, as though they'd been intimate hundreds of times before. They gave in to their emotions with such ease that she almost felt like she was outside of herself, watching another woman make love to him. For a few seconds, she wanted to claw the woman's eyes out. Then she heard him whisper "my Juliet" and "my baby girl" again and again, and she smiled as she realized that Maxi wasn't cheating on her. They tossed and turned on the bed in each other's arms, twisting the pink sheet all around them and creating a wild rustling noise that mimicked the incessant roar of the ocean. Her hair toppled on him like liquid gold and caressed his skin like gentle waves as she and Maxi made love with a rhythm like the tide rolling in and out. He moistened her body with tongue-kisses, refreshing her hot skin like cool waves splashing against the sun-soaked sand.

When they finally wore each other out, she rested her head on his chest, feeling its steady rise and fall while she and Maxi caught their breath. A cool breeze swirled into the room through the open window, gently ruffling the sheer pink curtains and refreshing Juliet's sweaty skin. She lifted her head to smile at him. The sun cut through the curtains and shone in Maxi's black-satin-sheet eyes, bringing out those beautiful brandy-brown flecks. She felt a little guilty for spending the entire morning in bed with a man instead of going outside and enjoying the gorgeous spring weather on her day off. Then again, she didn't feel guilty enough to get *out* of bed—not when Maxi Ward was in it with her.

"Baby girl—" He looked at her quietly for a moment and smiled. "You like it when I call you that, don't you? You light up whenever I say it, especially when we're making love. You get this dreamy look on your face. Your beautiful blue eyes get a little bluer. Your complexion gets a little pinker. You look so angelic that I almost feel ashamed for taking you to bed."

"Don't ever feel that way, Maxi."

He rolled on top of her and kissed her. "I said *almost*."

They kissed and kissed until her lips grew even sorer than they did on the first night that she slept with him. He reacquainted her with the innumerable ways a person can kiss, and this time each kiss tasted even better than before.

"Come away with me next weekend," he whispered passionately.

"Just make the reservations, anywhere," she answered in between their loud, hungry kisses. "You don't even need to ask me."

The clock in the hallway rang twelve times during their kissing fest.

"I have to leave in a few hours," he said, "to prepare for my dinner tonight with the English department at Stefano's."

"That's the one you go to every spring, right?"

"Yes. It's a social occasion, but we also use it as an opportunity to discuss lesson plans, changes in the mandatory reading material, etc. We jot down our thoughts in advance." He paused a second. "Say, do you work today?"

"No, I'm off. I'm going to do some painting."

"You never did tell me what you've been painting lately," he said.

"Couples slow dancing, kissing, walking on the beach—things like that."

"Did you paint us?"

"Not yet," she said. "I'd like to paint my mom and dad, but I don't have any pictures of him. After he died, my mom was so heartbroken that she couldn't bring herself to look at his pictures without sobbing, even years after his death. So she threw them all away."

Maxi held her close. "I'm sorry, baby girl. Your father would have loved you very much. He would have taken you to work and shown you off to his colleagues. He would have been so proud of your art talent and the way you're working to put yourself through art school some day." He kissed her forehead. "He would have been your first love, not me. I would have been jealous of him, because he would have had access to a part of your heart that would have always been closed off to me." He laughed softly. "And he would have hated me, because I just made love to his little girl. You would have had two men in your life, not one. So when you think about him, don't think in terms of what never was but what *would* have been if he'd lived. You two would have been close. Wrap yourself up in that feeling and hang on to it."

She smiled gratefully. "Thank you, Maxi."

They fell asleep in each other's arms for an hour or so. When they woke up, Maxi asked whether it would be all right if he used her shower. She told him to go right ahead. He squeezed her hand thankfully, brushing his thumb over her knuckles. They gazed at each other, their eyes brimming with passion.

With the sinuousness of a snake, they bathed each other slowly and sensually, then they made love while the water washed the suds off their bodies. He kissed her fleshy, round shoulders and the hollow area of her throat. She kissed his glistening biceps and pectoral muscles. His mouth plunged into her enormous breasts and endlessly explored their every supple curve as though he was venturing into territory that he hadn't already covered again and again the last two times they'd made love. He licked the rivulets of water that trickled down her cleavage while her hands eased their way down the nape of his neck and down his back. He kissed her nipples almost bashfully and then sucked on them as though he wanted to devour her. As usual, he had a unique way of blending passion with gentleness, a feeling so titillating to her that words couldn't begin to describe it. They looked at each other with loving eyes every now and then, keeping the intimacy alive while they made love with a fluidity that mimicked the cascading water. His wet, slicked back hair made him look sexy in an entirely different way, and she almost felt like she was making love to another man. She looked at him wide-eyed, suddenly feeling startled and a little ashamed.

"Maximilian?"

"What is it, baby girl?"

She breathed a sigh of relief and buried her face in his muscular neck, enjoying the beautiful rhythm of his pulse as it throbbed powerfully against her cheek. She kissed the beauty mark near his right eye and then kissed the water droplets that hung from the tips of his eyelashes.

"It's nothing," she said.

For an hour and a half they continued to make delirious love in the steamy shower, listening to each other's amorous groans and pants mingle merrily with the flow of hot water that beat against their skin. In her imagination, they were making love beneath a waterfall on their own private island. The light blue tile walls and blue shower curtain were lovely substitutes for the cloudless sky, and the luscious aroma of her shampoo and shower gel was reminiscent of flowers in a tropical paradise. The soapy, iridescent bubbles that she and Maxi had created resembled the foamy water in her opulent fantasy.

They returned to her bed and made love again while they kissed and licked some remaining water droplets off of each other. The shower had revitalized and invigorated them, strengthening their desire for one another. Besides, there was so much more that they could do in bed. He marveled at how soft and smooth her freshly showered skin was as he ran his hand over her outstretched body.

At three o'clock, he sighed and kissed her.

"I'm sorry, Juliet. I have to go."

He put on his underwear and pants, then he sat on the edge of the bed and took her hand in his. She came out from under the pink sheet and bedspread, and she crawled over to him on her hands and knees. He scooped her up in his arms, and she fell into his lap.

"So tell me, baby girl, where do you want to go next weekend?"

"Anywhere, Maxi. I don't care."

"How about a cozy inn in Cape May?"

She smiled. "My mom used to go there with Romy every December to see the town all dressed up in Christmas lights and decorations. I've never been there, but I've always wanted to go."

"Then we'll go."

She kissed him. "Maxi, the past two days we've spent together have been more precious to me than the twenty years I lived before this."

He laughed. "Please, don't get sappy on me, baby."

For the first time, she saw tears in his eyes in spite of his mocking remark. He lowered his head again as though he didn't want her to see. She kissed his cheek tenderly. That was her way of letting him know that she *did* see.

"So, Maxi, what were the other words you wanted to have engraved on my locket?"

He smiled. "All right, Jule, I'll tell you this much. I bought you another pendant, and the words are engraved on the back of it. I'll give it to you a month from now, on your twenty-first birthday."

"Oh, Maxi, thank you!" She hugged him. "I wasn't expecting anything like that."

"Jule baby, do you love me? I mean *really* love me?"

"Yes, of course I do. I love you in a dizzying and exhilarating kind of way, like I've lost the power to breathe." She smiled. "You're my infuriating sweetheart, Maxi. And it feels like every time I get angry at you, I end up loving you even more."

"Will you love me no matter what detestable thing I may say or do down the road, or what I may have already done that I might decide to tell you about some day?"

She looked into his eyes and touched his face. "Tell me, honey, what's worrying you?"

"There are a lot of things about me that you don't know, baby girl. Things I've done that I'm not proud of." His eyes looked vapid, as though he was putting up a wall that she didn't have the power to break down. "I love you very much, but sometimes I'm afraid to get too close to you. I think in the end, I'll disappoint you because I didn't turn out to be the man you thought I was."

Her heart was slamming against her chest. That wall injected more fear into her heart than anything ever had before, but at the same time, she loved that he was opening up to her and expressing his true feelings. She held him close, knowing how fragile this moment was, because whatever she said could make or break her future with him.

"Maxi honey, I'm sorry for being so hard on you last night. I need you to give me another chance to show you that I'll *listen* to you, not judge you, if and when you decide to confide in me. And I promise that I'll never walk away from you again. I'll never leave you. As long as you're sorry for whatever you did in the past, then that's good enough for me."

She embraced him and whispered again that she loved him. When they were face to face again, his eyes were luminous and spirited once more. She sealed her little monologue with a deep kiss, and that kiss led to a long smooching session. As he held her close, her giant breasts pressed against his bare chest. He started to pant, and not long after that, he unzipped his slacks. They fell on the bed together and made love one last time before he had to leave, taking turns being on top as they tried to quench their desire for each other. After forty-five minutes of rapturous sex, he ran his hand over his still damp hair as he wearily climbed out of bed and let out a few exasperated breaths.

"All right, lovergirl." He grinned. "Now I *really* have to go."

He pulled on his clothes, then he picked up her locket from the nightstand and put it around her neck. She slipped into a pink terrycloth robe, tying the sash tightly around her waist, and walked him to the front door. They stepped out on the porch and shared one last kiss, an ultra long one. She wished that her neighbors would come out of hiding so that she could show the rest of the world how much she loved him.

After their lips parted, she and Maxi noticed a red Mercedes in the street, waiting for the red light to turn green. It was the first sign of human life that she had noticed on Clover Lane in weeks, but that wasn't the only thing that caught her attention. The driver's violet-blue eyes were frightfully fixed on the two lovers. Juliet gulped nervously.

The light turned green, and Miranda gunned the engine and sped away.

CHAPTER SIXTEEN

"Dammit, Jules, now you're gonna go off with this guy and spend the entire weekend with him?"

Vienna slammed her glass on Romy's white kitchen countertop as she and Juliet helped Romy to clean up after dinner. The glass made a loud thud, and a few drops of mineral water splashed out, hitting Romy in the face.

"Sorry, Romy."

"We just want to get away from here and be alone together," Juliet said amidst the clanking of silverware against Romy's daisy-speckled china as she cleared the dining room table.

Romy grabbed her homemade chocolate cake from the refrigerator, some plates and forks, and headed to the dining room table. She and Vienna sat at the table opposite Juliet, and the trio sliced up the cake. Romy had set a beautiful table, complete with vanilla-scented candles atop Waterford crystal candle holders, a flower arrangement of daisies and daffodils, and a beige tablecloth that matched the color of Romy's summer dress and the Lenox china animal figurines in the curio cabinet behind Juliet.

"Today I saw tears in his eyes for the very first time," Juliet said.

Vienna's eyes widened. "Maxi Ward had tears in his eyes?"

"I told him how much I've cherished our time together, and he started to cry. He lowered his head like he didn't want me to see." Juliet closed her eyes and smiled softly as her nostrils savored the scrumptious scent of vanilla, remembering that Maxi had loved it on her last night.

"Well, what do you know, the man has a sensitive side," Vienna said, wolfing down a huge forkful of cake.

Juliet showed Vienna and Romy the eighteen-karat gold chain that Maxi had given her and the engraving on the back of her gold heart locket.

"That's beautiful, Jule," Romy said.

"Maxi is the only man I'll ever love."

Vienna stared at her. "You spent the whole day in bed with him, didn't you?"

"Vienna!" Juliet motioned her head toward Romy.

"Don't worry, Romy's not going to run to her priest and tell him."

"Romy," Juliet said, "try not to think of it as premarital sex." She smiled warmly. "You know that in my heart, I *am* married to Maxi."

"You don't even care that Mom's dead," Vienna said with a few tears in her voice. "You're too wrapped up with Maxi to care. Sometimes I think you only cried at her funeral so Maxi would put his arms around you."

Juliet frowned. "I can't believe you would actually say that or even think it. I may not go to her grave every other day like you do, but I loved her, too. Maxi didn't rape her or anyone else. How do you think Cassandra would feel if she knew you thought her father was a rapist?"

"That's rich, Jules. You're her friend. How do you think she feels knowing you're screwing him? Besides, she doesn't care what I think of him. She's in love with me!"

Juliet bolted backward in her chair. "What the hell did you say?"

"Cassandra Ward, our friend for the past five years, is in love with me."

Juliet's eyes widened. "She told you this?"

"Yes, she did, yesterday. I talked to her and tried to smooth things over, and we're still friends. But she's hurting, and I don't know whether things will ever be quite the same."

"Why didn't you call me at the boutique yesterday and tell me? I could have gotten together with her after work and tried to console her."

"I figured you'd made plans with Maxi," Vienna said.

"But I want to help her."

"You want to help someone, Jules? Help *me*. Give me Miranda Key's address. I want to talk to her."

"No!"

Suddenly Romy's dark eyes sprung wide open. She looked like a woman who was trapped in a room with sewer rats crawling all over the floor and furniture. The mere mention of Miranda Key drained the blood from her cheeks and made her face stark white. She looked a little frightening against the glowing candlelight, like she belonged in some cheesy horror movie.

"What's wrong, Romy?" Vienna asked.

"You girls know Miranda Key?"

"I do," Juliet said. "She came into the boutique yesterday and bought a nightgown. I mentioned Maxi's name, and she freaked out. She said Maxi raped her back in high school."

"He didn't. Don't listen to anything that woman says."

"You knew Miranda from school?" Vienna asked.

"Not very well but well enough to know that she's a liar. She hates Maxi because of some things he said about her and her sister."

"What did he say?" Juliet asked.

"Well, Miranda had a reputation, see."

Juliet nodded. "I know. She admitted to that."

"And apparently her sister had one, too," Romy said. "She was at the high school five years before Miranda. Maxi told his friends, purely in jest, that Miranda was moonlighting as a hooker, and that she was making a porno movie during summer vacation. He said she was following in her sister's footsteps."

Vienna nodded. "I can picture Maxi saying that."

"So this turned into a full-blown rumor that spread throughout the school like wildfire. The teachers heard it. Some people actually took it seriously. I heard some guys even ask her how much she charged for an hour of her services. They wanted to know what kinds of services she performed. Did she take on two guys at once? Did she give oral sex? Did she use handcuffs or blindfolds? A couple of them wanted to know whether her sister was still a hooker or was she a madam now. Then there was the alleged porno movie. Guys asked her whether the sex was real or simulated. Since they were underage, they wanted to know whether Miranda could get them into the theater because she knew them. They said she was probably going to win an award that year for best actress in an erotic film."

"Geez, the guys were really that cruel?" Vienna asked.

"You don't know the half of it," Romy said. "Then somehow Miranda's parents got wind of the rumor, and they made her go to a therapist who specialized in sexual compulsive disorder. They even threatened to throw her out of the house if she didn't change her ways. I suppose they knew about her reputation, otherwise they probably never would have believed Maxi's jokes. It got to the point where Miranda just couldn't take it anymore. One day I was in the girls' bathroom, in one of the stalls, and I heard the door whoosh open and Miranda started cursing and slamming her fist against the stall doors. She hissed, 'Damn that Maxi Ward. I hate him! Who the hell does he think he is? I'll find some way to get back at him, no matter what I have to do. I'll even fix it so everyone thinks he raped me, if that's what it takes.' And then I heard her sob uncontrollably for several minutes. Deep, ragged sobs—like the sobs of a girl who really *had* been raped. It was very sad. The despair in her voice was so severe that it practically brought me to tears. I actually felt pity for her, even though she was scheming to get back at Maxi."

Vienna shook her head in disbelief. "What a story."

"That's not all. I heard her sniffling and blowing her nose, then there was a period of silence. I thought she'd left the bathroom, so I opened the stall door and stepped out. But Miranda was still there, her back to me. When she heard me come out, she slowly turned around and peered over her shoulder at me, giving me a look so bitterly cold it would have made even the devil quake in fear. So I kept my mouth shut about what I'd heard her say. I was afraid that if I'd testified in Maxi's defense, she'd have come after me. To this very day, Miranda Key is the only person who has ever evoked such immense fear and compassion in me at the same time."

"She told me that Maxi got in trouble for doing speed in the quad and having sex in the girls' locker room and in a teacher's classroom," Juliet said.

Romy laughed. "Maxi never would have done any of those things! Are you kidding me? Miranda herself was the star of those sex scenes. Oh, that girl was unbelievable! And those were only two of the places in school where she had sex. There were lots of other places where she didn't get caught. Students saw her having sex in the quad, in the girls' bathroom, in the boys' bathroom, under the bleachers in the gym, in the swimming pool, and on the lunch table in the cafeteria last period of the day. And this was just in her sophomore year. She was lucky none of those students reported her. That girl just couldn't help herself. She loved sex, way too much. Sometimes I think she knew someone was watching her all those times, and she enjoyed it. She liked putting on a show and entertaining people, otherwise she never would have risked doing it in school so many times. Did Maxi tell you she got pregnant in her junior year?"

"No, he didn't."

"She quit school to have the baby, and she moved to New York. I didn't know she came back here."

"Who was the father of her baby?" Vienna asked.

"No one knew," Romy said. "I wonder whether *she* knew, after all those lovers she had."

"I think I should go back to her apartment and give her a piece of my mind," Juliet said.

"You've been to her apartment?" Romy's voice was so high-pitched that it grated against Juliet's eardrums.

"Oh, yeah, you should see it! Red everywhere. I couldn't wait to get the hell out of there."

Vienna smiled. "Jules thinks Miranda slaughtered a bunch of people and painted everything in the apartment with their blood."

"Well, I don't think she has it in her to *kill* anybody," Romy said. "But I'm telling you right now, don't go back there anymore. Don't call her. Just stay away from her. Especially you, Vienna. Trust me, you don't want to cross this woman. She's a perpetual liar."

Juliet was afraid to mention that Miranda had spotted her and Maxi on the porch earlier that day, and she now knew where the twins lived.

"The femme fatale of Tiger Lily High, hm?" Vienna said. "And all these years we thought Tiger Lily was a sweet, wholesome little town."

"If only," Romy said. "But you can rest easy knowing that Maxi didn't rape her."

"He thinks our dad raped our mom! Do you believe the nerve of that man?"

"Maxi said that?" Romy looked very solemn and offended all of a sudden. "No, your father never would have done that. He was a wonderful man, a gentle and compassionate soul. Maxi didn't know him. He never would have said that if he'd known him."

"All I know is that the man she mentioned in her letter was someone she trusted," Juliet said.

"But he didn't rape her."

"How do you know this, Romy?"

"I just do."

Juliet leaned forward, so concerned that she almost knocked over her plate with her elbow. "Romy, please tell us what you know. We can't go on with this hanging over our heads."

"Then let it go. Forget about it and move on with your lives."

"Let it go? Romy, our mother killed herself because of a mysterious involvement with a potentially dangerous man."

"Who's the man and what did he do to her, Romy?" Vienna asked.

"And why are you protecting him? Your best friend is dead because of him!"

"There are some things you're better off not knowing," Romy said in a quiet, sinister voice.

"Oh, my God, he did rape Mom," Vienna breathed.

"No, he didn't."

"But he abused her in some way?" Juliet asked.

"No, you misunderstood Felicity's note. It wasn't an abusive relationship." Romy hesitated before saying any more. "It was a forbidden one."

"Forbidden how? The man was married?"

"No," Romy said.

"Were their families on bad terms with each other?" Vienna asked.

"No, it wasn't like that."

The more that Romy spoke, the quieter her voice became. She wouldn't even look at the twins. Her eyes stayed focused on the flowers in the center of the table.

"I'll tell you," she said. Her voice was a weary whisper now. She rubbed her eyes and took a deep breath as though she'd been beaten down, because they were forcing this out of her. She closed her eyes and shook her head very slowly. "I promised her I wouldn't tell you. God forgive me." She opened her eyes and looked at them. "He was a priest."

"A priest?" Vienna laughed. "Our mother had an affair with a priest? No way."

"He was twenty-nine. He'd taken his vows just six or seven months before the affair began."

"When *did* the affair begin?" Juliet asked.

"She met him when she was sixteen, the year before your uncle Sonny died."

The twins furrowed their brows in confusion. "We had an uncle?"

"Yes, your mom's big brother. I'll take you to his grave some time. He and Felicity were close. He was only twenty-six when he died. He was shot in the middle of a bank hold-up. His killer went to prison with a lifelong sentence, but he didn't last very long in there. Some of the other inmates ganged up on him in the shower, and they beat him to death."

"What does this have to do with the priest?" Vienna asked.

"Sonny was friends with a young priest who had taken his vows the year before. After Sonny died, Felicity was devastated. She leaned on the priest for support because they'd both been close to Sonny. They struck up a very strong friendship that eventually deepened into love. They tried to be discreet about the affair, not only because he was a priest, but also because she was only seventeen and he was twenty-nine. If someone had found out that they were having sex, he could have been thrown in jail for statutory rape."

"Was this affair going on even while she was married?" Juliet asked.

Romy hesitated again for a minute or so. "Felicity wasn't married. Everything she told you about your father being a legal clerk and dying in a fire was just a story she made up for your benefit. She wanted you to grow up with traditional family values, believing that she and your dad were married, but it was a lie. She didn't want to tell you the truth, that your father was—"

Vienna gaped at her but didn't say anything. Juliet herself was afraid to speak. She didn't need to. She'd already anticipated what Romy's next words would be.

"The priest is your father."

Vienna sat at the table in a daze, peering into space like she was trying to make sense of the whole bizarre thing. The light in her silver-blue eyes was fading, like she was dying by degrees. She looked like a worn out old dog or cat that was about to be put to sleep. Juliet felt so sad for her. She didn't expect Vienna to be speechless. She thought she'd dismiss this stunning revelation as a joke again, or maybe throw a fit and yell. But Vienna simply sat there looking lost and weak, apparently too exhausted to exert any kind of reaction. It was downright pitiful. Juliet had never seen her look so emotionally drained. Vienna had always been so tough, so fierce. Not anymore, not now. Too much stress. The girl had shut down.

"Our father is alive?" Juliet said. "And no one told us?"

"It wouldn't have done you any good," Romy said.

"How can you say that?"

"What would you rather live with?" Romy asked. "The image of your father as a man who died in a fire, or a priest who couldn't even be a real father to you?"

"The truth would have been nice. If our mom wasn't brave enough to tell us, then you should have. What's his name? What parish does he serve at?"

"St. Anthony's, my parish. His name is Victor Desiderio."

"What is he like?" Juliet asked. "Does he look like us?"

"He's a very refined gentleman in his fifties with red hair like Felicity and a fair complexion. He's a good-hearted man. Gives the most inspirational sermons I've ever heard. Felicity told him all about you girls. She showed him pictures of you."

"I can't believe he's really alive," Vienna said, still staring into space looking dumbstruck.

"Was the affair going on right up until she killed herself?" Juliet asked.

"No, it ended after she found out she was pregnant," Romy said. "Then they agreed to remain friends. I think in her heart she was hoping he would leave the priesthood for her, but she never dared to ask him. She was too gracious to do that. She wanted him to make that decision on his own. But he asked her to keep him abreast of what was going on in your lives."

"So what did he have to do with Mom's suicide?" Juliet asked.

"Victor Desiderio is the only man your mother ever loved. She fell in love with him when she was seventeen. She died when she was thirty-eight, and right up until the day she died, she loved him and only him. She was tormented inside, because she wanted to tell you about him, but she thought you'd be ashamed of her for having an affair with a priest."

"But if it hadn't been for that affair, we wouldn't be here," Juliet said.

"That's what I told her, but it didn't do any good. She was such a lonely woman when she was apart from him. Watching her grieve for him was such a painful experience to live through, because that's exactly what she was doing. Grieving, as though he really were dead all these years. She had no idea how to exist without him. She used to call him her soulmate. After they broke up, she just couldn't open up her heart to anyone else."

"So Victor was the reason why she killed herself?"

Romy nodded. "It had to be. I saw how much she suffered and how long. I honestly don't know how she managed to hide it from you all these years."

"What did she mean in the letter when she said that he violated her trust?" Vienna asked.

"Deep down Felicity resented the fact that he came into her life, made her fall in love with him, and then ended the affair. Like I said, I think in her heart, she really wanted and expected him to leave the priesthood for her after he found out she was pregnant. When he didn't, she was heartbroken. She felt like he'd abandoned her."

"So when she checked herself out of this world, it was like she chose to die for him," Vienna said, "instead of choosing to live for us."

"Now wait a second," Romy said. "Felicity loved you girls. Don't ever forget that. But her depression was like a maze that she couldn't find a way out of. First her brother died when she was only a girl of seventeen. That made her so furious at the world that she wanted to escape from it. In the beginning she chose hard liquor as her method of escape. Gin, whiskey, vodka—you name it, she tried it. Lots of it. When that didn't do the trick, she started on cocaine."

"Mom? You're kidding me!"

"I'm dead serious," Romy said. "I was terrified for her. I thought she was going to become addicted. But then Victor began to spend time with her, and he tried to help her. And she tried to help him, in what small way she could, because he was grieving, too. And then they fell in love, and *he* became her addiction. But sadly, she had to give him up, too, just like the booze and the drugs." She sighed and shook her head. "She could never deal with loss and grief. They overwhelmed her. In the end, that's what killed her. And as for her method of suicide, I think she chose a gunshot because that was how her brother had died, and she wanted her final act on earth to be connected to him somehow. She wanted to die the same way that he had. It gave her a little consolation, I suppose. That was how much she'd missed him."

"Why couldn't she talk to us about all this?" Juliet asked.

"She didn't want to burden you with her troubles, because you had enough to deal with, living without a father. I'm sorry, girls, for everything. We never meant to hurt you or betray you. She only wanted to protect you, and I only wanted to honor her wishes. She confided in me for twenty years. I could never turn my back on her and betray that confidence. I hope you'll try to understand."

Now Vienna was looking blankly at the aquarium on the bay window in the dining room. Juliet knew she always turned to the bright blue and red Siamese fighting fish for solace. Maybe that was because Vienna herself was a fighter, so she felt she connected with them on some level. Her shoulder-length blond hair was parted on the side and swept over one eye so that half her face was hidden. So were Vienna's thoughts. Juliet only wished that she could read them. She wondered whether Vienna would ever be able to forgive Romy, considering the special connection they'd always shared. Juliet prepared herself for an emotional eruption.

"Are there any more secrets, Romy?" Vienna asked quietly.

"No."

Vienna turned in her chair to face Romy and looked her squarely in the eyes. "Romy, if there *is* anything else, now is the time to get it out in the open. No more secrets. No more lies. No more protecting the poor little innocent Mann sisters. No more honoring dead people's wishes. Jules and I need to know the truth about everything that involves us, no matter how insignificant some of the details may seem. Now, can you swear to us that there are no more secrets?"

Romy looked right into Vienna's eyes. "There are no more secrets, I swear."

Vienna's eyes stayed stuck to Romy's. Juliet started to sweat through the long, creepy silence as she and Romy waited for Vienna to say something.

Finally Vienna nodded. "Okay," she said in a voice so soft that Juliet barely heard her.

Juliet breathed deeply, surprised and thankful that Vienna had decided to work through this situation calmly and without melodrama.

For now at least.

CHAPTER SEVENTEEN

Romy shocked the girls by bringing Victor Desiderio to the house the very next morning. Apparently she wanted to give the father and daughters some time alone, because she left immediately after introducing Victor, excusing herself by saying that she wanted to make the ten A.M. Sunday mass.

Victor was just as Romy had described—a distinguished looking middle-aged man with red hair like Felicity. Juliet remembered how her mother used to say that when couples looked alike, she believed they were meant for each other. Juliet wondered about that from time to time. She and Maxi didn't look anything alike.

Victor sat in the chair beside the sofa, looking very sullen and not saying anything at first, just clasping his hands together solemnly and avoiding the twins' gazes. Obviously he felt just as uneasy as they did, although he didn't exactly look like he wanted to be some place else. He just looked like he was searching his mind for the right words to start off the conversation. He'd probably played out this big moment in his head countless times over the years, wondering what his daughters' voices sounded like and what kinds of questions they'd ask him. Now that the moment was here, his mind had frozen, perhaps, and everything he'd planned to say had evaporated.

Finally Victor looked up at them. "I'm very sorry that you lost your mother. It's such a tragedy. She was so young. How are you both doing?"

"Getting by," Vienna said. "Romy and Cassandra have been here for us."

"Cassandra Ward is our best friend," Juliet said. "Her father Maximilian is my boyfriend."

"So you have a support system," Victor said. "I'm glad. I realize this meeting is awkward for all of us, and I know you're both probably confused and angry about the decision your mother and I made, not to tell you everything."

"Are you angry at *us*?" Vienna asked. "Because we wanted to meet you?"

"No, of course not. No, I'm very grateful for this opportunity."

"Do you have to get back to St. Anthony's to say mass?" Juliet asked.

"Not for a couple more hours. I'm saying the twelve-thirty mass today." He smiled just a touch. "You girls look like your mother."

Vienna looked at Juliet in surprise, then back at Victor. "We do?"

"No one's ever told us that before," Juliet said.

"You have her eyes." His blue eyes became watery. "I miss her very much."

"We miss her, too," Vienna said. "So does Romy."

"Romy is a wonderful person. I think we knew your mother better than most other people ever did."

He was sitting forward in the chair with his elbows on his knees and his hands clasped together again like he was in a deep state of meditation.

"I am truly sorry," he said. "For everything."

"For what it's worth," Juliet said, "I'm glad that everything is finally out in the open."

He nodded. "I only hope that one day I'll be able to help you understand why I left her, and you. And I want to tell you about your uncle Sonny, some day. It's hard to talk about him sometimes, and it was hard for your mother, too. Maybe by not saying anything it was her way of trying to put the past behind her. She had a hard time reflecting on her happy memories of him. It was too painful for her, and it only made her miss him more." He looked at the twins. "I loved your mother. She had a side to her that she kept hidden from the rest of the world."

"And from us," Vienna said.

"She wasn't an easy person to get to know, but once you did know her, it was virtually impossible not to love her in some way. And I'd like you to know that even though you weren't conceived in a unity of marriage, you were conceived in love. Felicity and I would have gotten married if circumstances had been different."

He paused a moment, lowering his head in quiet reflection. Juliet sensed that he blamed himself for Felicity's death, and he was probably trying to find some way to forgive himself.

She wanted to cry for this broken man who she didn't even know, for this stranger who was her father.

"Please don't be angry at your mother," he said. "Pray for her. I do."

The telephone rang. Vienna waved her hand in its direction. "The machine will get it."

On the third ring, the machine picked up. Cassandra left the message, "Vienna, Jule, call me as soon as you get this." She sounded frantic, and Juliet heard her sniffle once or twice.

CHAPTER EIGHTEEN

Maxi had been killed by a hit-and-run driver last night while he was crossing the street from Stefano's restaurant after his dinner with the English department. The driver sped away too quickly for any of Maxi's colleagues to catch the license plate number. Maxi died instantly.

Juliet and Vienna cancelled their plans to take a day trip together. Romy made the funeral arrangements while the twins spent most of the afternoon with Cassandra at her place. She couldn't stop crying. Juliet, on the other hand, was in too much shock to cry yet. She didn't want to think about having to attend his funeral, because the last funeral she went to was her mother's three weeks ago. Maxi had been her lifeline then.

Who would be her lifeline now?

The world without Maxi was a bleak, colorless place. She couldn't even bring herself to look at Cassandra anymore, because Cassandra was only an extension of Maxi and not Maxi himself. Juliet felt so alone and empty inside, because she ached for him but she just couldn't bring herself to let it all out. It didn't seem real yet. Still, she knew she had to talk to someone, and that someone needed to be a man. That was the only way that she could feel connected to Maxi again. And that man needed to be someone who also understood loss.

114 · Lisa Marie Pellegrini

She remembered Romy mentioning once that the priests at St. Anthony's Church heard confessions from four-thirty till five o'clock on Sundays. Juliet took a chance that Victor might be the assigned priest today, so she arrived at the church at five sharp, hoping she'd catch him leaving the confessionals so she could speak to him.

St. Anthony's was a small tan and white stone church, just six or seven blocks from Clover Lane. The dark wooden pews were empty, and the church was so quiet that she could hear herself breathe. The altar was a beautiful grey and white marble. Only one candle was lit in front of the Blessed Mother statue, and Juliet noticed a red light shining at one of the two confessionals in the front of the church. She assumed that whoever was confessing their sins must have lit the candle beforehand. She could tell that the person was a woman, because she heard her garbled voice through the wooden door of the confessional. And yes, Victor was the priest on duty. His name was engraved in gold on the confessional door.

Juliet admired the rainbow-hued stained glass on the sides of the church while she waited, wondering just how many sins this lady had to confess and what kind of advice Victor was giving her. Finally the door knob turned, and an elegant looking middle-aged brunette woman in a white skirt and pink blouse came out. She breathed deeply, looking frazzled and relieved all at once. Maybe she hadn't been to confession in a long time, and this had been a nerve-wracking experience for her. She knelt down in the first pew, made the sign of the cross, and clasped her hands together in prayer. A few minutes later, Victor came out and proceeded down the aisle, greeting Juliet with a smile as soon as his blue eyes met hers.

"Hello, Juliet."

"Hi, Father."

"Call me Victor. Are you all right?"

"I'm fine," she said. "I know you have to get ready for the five-thirty mass, but may I talk to you for a few minutes?"

"Of course." He sat in the pew beside her. "How are you holding up?"

"Maxi's death has raised some issues in my mind that I feel I need to explore."

"What kinds of issues?" He was talking in a hushed voice now, as though treating this conversation like a confession.

She breathed deeply, trying to relax before she told him what she was about to tell him. "Maxi and I loved each other very much, Victor." She swallowed hard. "We slept together."

A sliver of a shadow crossed his face. Suddenly it was like he was juggling two roles, that of a father who didn't want to hear about his daughter sleeping with a man as well as a priest who didn't like hearing about premarital sex.

"I suppose I'm looking for answers, Victor. I know that the Catholic Church considers premarital sex a sin. But what I'd like to know is, could Maxi's death factor into it at all?"

"How do you mean?"

"Well, now that he's gone," she said, "I'll never again have the chance to share my love with him in that way. So my question is this: was what I did with him still considered wrong?"

She knew she could have approached another priest for guidance, but Victor was her father, and he knew exactly what she was going through. Maybe he would go easy on her. After all, her heart didn't really want an honest answer to her question anyway, even if her brain did. She felt a little guilty for using their father-daughter connection as leverage, but didn't all Daddy's girls bat their eyes innocently and tug on Daddy's heartstrings so they'd get their way?

"You know I can't be objective about this, Juliet."

I can't be objective. Jule, I can't let you into my Shakespeare class, because I can't be objective about your work.

Maxi's words pulsated in her brain. Not even twenty-four hours had passed since he died, and already she missed his soft but manly voice and everything about him that made him Maxi Ward. She missed hearing him call her "baby girl." She yearned to feel his kiss again and the gentle way that he used to pull her into his arms and console her whenever she was sad. If only she'd known that their goodbye kiss on her front porch yesterday had been a goodbye kiss in every sense of the word. She wondered whether Miranda was his killer. Maxi's colleagues had told the police that they didn't get a look at the hit-and-run driver. It was too dark outside. All they noticed was that the car was red, but they couldn't be sure that it was a Mercedes.

Victor looked at Juliet warmly. "Then again, maybe you don't *want* an objective answer."

"I would appreciate any answer you can give me."

He nodded. "So you and Maxi had sexual relations. Talk to me. Tell me about it."

Talk to me, Jule. Tell me what's wrong.

It seemed like every time Victor opened his mouth, Maxi's words came rushing out. She closed her eyes and took a deep breath, trying to regain her composure. Maybe it was true what everyone said about girls chasing after men like their fathers.

"Juliet?"

She opened her eyes. "Hm?"

"Are you okay?"

"I'm fine, Victor, thanks." She took a moment to gather her thoughts together. "Maxi brought out a side of me that I never even knew existed. He was my only lover. We were only together a few times, but during those times, we made love over and over again. That's how strong our desire for each other was. It had been building up for almost four years." She paused a minute, waiting for his reaction, but he stayed silent and waited for her to continue. "Before I met Maxi, I never pictured myself spending half the day in bed with a man, making love to him the way you see it in the movies. I never imagined that I'd have sex with him in the shower—for an hour and a half, no less. Before I met Maxi, I suppose I never even thought I would *like* sex so much. But with him, it was so easy to love, because *he* was so easy to love. He was right. He said there was a beast inside of me. And of course he was the only man who knew how to bring it out." She smiled a little shamefully, suddenly remembering who she was talking to. "I never pictured myself sitting in a church and talking to a priest about these things."

"That's all right. You're doing fine. Take your time."

Take your time. Juliet had heard Romy say that to Vienna whenever Vienna had something preying on her mind.

"Victor, those moments that Maxi and I shared were physically pleasurable beyond words. But it was because I loved him so much. He had a sweetness about him and a gentleness that the rest of the world didn't see, but I saw it. He was beautiful and wonderful, and I didn't care about his flaws and his checkered past. I wanted to marry him some day and have his children, more than anything else in the world." She turned towards Victor a little more in the pew, in case another priest or a parishioner came walking down the aisle. "Victor,

I'm not sorry for sleeping with him. If I hadn't, I'd have to go through the rest of my life wondering what the experience would have been like. I'm grateful that I know, and that I can always look back on those times and treasure the memories."

He nodded. She could see that he understood what she meant without coming right out and disclosing details about his own relationship with Felicity. And she decided that it wasn't her place to ask him either. After they'd gotten to know each other better, and if—or when—the time was right, she assumed that he would tell her and Vienna about it when he was ready.

"I guess what I'm trying to say, Victor, is that I know what I did was wrong, technically. But considering the unique circumstances surrounding it, was it really *wrong*?"

"Juliet, do you want the truth?"

"Yes, I do."

"Are you sure?" he asked.

She hesitated now.

"Juliet, I can't answer your question until I know for sure whether you're prepared to hear the truth. Or do you simply want me to tell you what you want to hear?"

She looked down, not knowing how to respond.

"I'm not trying to be hard on you," he said very kindly. "Please understand that."

"I know. I'm the one who's making this hard for *you*, and I'm sorry. But isn't it remotely possible that the truth and what I want to hear just might be the same thing?"

He shook his head. "I'm sorry, dear. Believe me, I do feel for you. You've suffered an enormous loss, but I won't lie to you as a means of consoling you. I hope you understand."

"I do. I'm sorry that I put you in that position."

"That's all right," he said. "Please don't feel offended. I do want to be here for you in any other way I can. I think we should talk about this again after you've had time to process your thoughts. I know you're still in shock. Give yourself time to let everything sink in."

"I promised him I would never leave him." She lowered her head, wishing for tears, hoping they would cleanse her inside somehow and wash away some of her pain. "He left me instead. I miss him so much, but I can't cry for him. The tears just won't come."

"They will, in time." He took her hand in his. "It will happen when you least expect it, just like so many other things in life."

She looked up at him, stunned because she was feeling her father's touch for the very first time, the father she never even knew was alive until last night. It was an experience she thought she would never have the privilege to know, and yet now it was actually happening to her. For four years she had depended on Maxi for fatherly support, and now, sitting beside her and holding her hand was the man she'd been yearning for all that time. It was almost as though Maxi's spirit had sent Victor to her, as crazy as that probably sounded.

"You know," Victor said, "your mother and I remained friends for many years, and we used to talk about you and Vienna—about your talents, achievements, and aspirations. She mentioned that you're an artist, and that you're saving money to go to art school one day." He smiled. "I'd like to see your work some time."

"Sure. Stop by whenever you have a chance."

"I will, thanks," he said. "And you know, I met Maxi once. Romy and your mother went to high school with him, and Romy introduced me to him. He seemed very nice."

"So you and Romy are pretty close?"

"Yes, we're good friends," he said.

"She's been wonderful to me and Vienna all these years. She was such a big help to my mom when we were growing up, babysitting us and helping my mom take care of us when we got sick. Helping us with our homework. And that doesn't even begin to cover everything she's done for us."

He nodded. "Romy has a good heart."

"Victor, do you know about what Maxi did to my mother?"

"Yes, I do."

"You're probably wondering why I still loved him after that," she said.

"Romy told me he turned his life around. That's all that matters."

She nodded. "Maxi and I were planning to go away together next weekend, to Cape May. We were really looking forward to it."

"I'm sorry, Juliet." Victor smiled softly. "Your mother used to go there with Romy."

"At Christmas time, I know."

"And they also visited Stone Harbor and Avalon," he said. "There are some nice art galleries there. You should go some time and maybe bring your paintings along."

"I'd like that."

Victor looked at his watch. "I'm sorry, Juliet, I have to get ready for mass."

"Well, thank you for taking time to talk to me."

"Oh, I enjoyed it," he said. "I'm looking forward to seeing you again. I intend to go to Maxi's funeral, by the way."

She nodded. "I appreciate that."

He studied her locket. "You bought that necklace when you graduated high school, right?"

She was shocked. "You know about that?"

"Your mother told me. And I suppose Maxi's picture is inside."

"Yes, it is," she said. "But I never told my mother *that*."

He smiled. "Lucky guess." He stood up in the pew. "Take care of yourself, Juliet."

"I will."

"By the way," he said, "with all of the tragedy and sadness we've lived through today, I neglected to tell you something."

"Oh?"

He touched her cheek. "You're a very beautiful young woman. Kind and loving."

"Thank you, Victor."

"Maxi was a lucky man."

He bent over and kissed her tenderly on the cheek. Her heart almost stopped. Here was another act of affection that she hadn't expected. She looked up at him, speechless. His eyes looked misty but happy and proud at the same time, as though he'd been waiting forever for this moment, too. She hated that she couldn't make her lips or her body move, because she wanted so much to say or do something in return. But the smile on his face and the depth of emotion in his watery blue eyes suggested that he understood without her having to say or do anything at all.

And then he left her.

Three acts of affection, all in the time frame of just one conversation. She closed her eyes, took a deep breath of surprise and exhilaration, and gently laid her hand on the cheek that he had touched. Then she thought about the kiss, that precious kiss that she'd longed for ever since she was a child. She had to keep reminding herself that he was her father and that her father had actually done those wonderful things. She savored the whole experience and played it over and over again in her mind, letting the moment last just a little longer each time.

Then she remembered what Maxi had told her—that if she'd known her father, he would have loved her and they would have shared a special bond—and suddenly it was like Maxi was right there with her. But then again, of course he was, in spirit if not in body. She smiled softly.

Ten minutes later she found herself still sitting in the pew and still shocked that it really happened.

All of it.

CHAPTER NINETEEN

"Jules, where have you been?" Vienna asked.

"Out driving, to clear my head a little," Juliet said as she shut the front door and joined Vienna on the sofa. "Before that I paid Victor a visit at St. Anthony's."

She fanned herself with an art magazine that was on the coffee table. The white cotton summer dress she was wearing didn't make her feel any more comfortable. Summer seemed to be coming early this year. It was only the middle of May, but it was already eighty-five degrees outside. She'd felt much cooler at St. Anthony's because it was air conditioned.

"We need to turn on the air," she said.

"No sense doing it now. We're sleeping at Cassandra's." Vienna looked like she didn't even need the air conditioner. She was wearing a black tank top with a matching skort (shorts that looked like a skirt), and her hair was piled on top of her head in an upsweep and secured with black crystal bobby pins. "So what did you and Victor talk about?"

"Me and Maxi. I like Victor. He's very sweet."

"Seems very serious, like Romy. But he *is* a priest, so I guess that makes sense."

"Vien, should we be angry at him for leaving Mom and us?"

Vienna shrugged. "I don't know. I guess so. But I'm tired of being angry. He's our blood. We don't have any more of that left. Maybe we should look at it this way: we lost our mother, but we got our father back. Maybe it evens out, in a sense."

Juliet nodded. "I invited him to stop by some time. Is that all right with you?"

"Sure."

Juliet smiled faintly. "He thinks I'm beautiful."

"He's supposed to. He's your father."

"He knew all about my locket," Juliet said. "He wants to see my drawings."

Vienna looked like she was suppressing a smile as she studied Juliet. "You're already hooked on him, aren't you?"

Juliet smiled again. "He kissed me on the cheek."

"Right there in church?"

Juliet nodded. "No one else was around."

"Look at you. You're blushing!"

"I am not."

Vienna was smiling outwardly now. "Jules is in love with Daddy. And it only took twenty years." She touched Juliet's arm. "You know I'm not trying to be mean or vulgar. I think it's sweet that you're already taken with him."

"Well, I don't really know him yet."

"But you will, in time," Vienna said.

"I hope so." Juliet smiled when she thought about his kiss.

"I can't believe this, Jules. You're glowing!"

"Getting that kiss was the happiest moment of my life—and it happened on the saddest day of my life. Funny, isn't it?"

"Yeah, life is a mystery all right," Vienna said. "So what happened after he kissed you? Did you kiss him, too?"

"No, I was so shocked that I couldn't think straight. I was totally dumbfounded."

"And you didn't hug him either?" Vienna asked.

"No."

"Aw, that's a shame! Well, maybe when you see him again you can make up for it."

"I will," Juliet said.

Now that Vienna had mentioned it, Juliet wished she *had* embraced him, just to feel him in her arms to prove to herself that he really was alive and well. But even without the hug, just feeling his kiss and his hand on her cheek gave her more pleasure than she could ever put into words. She felt as excited as she did on the morning after she slept with Maxi—even happier because what had seemed like the impossible turned out to be very much possible. Maxi had told her that her father would have been her first love, had she grown up knowing him, but now the reverse seemed to be coming true. So she was going to have to get used to the backward feeling of it all and learn how to love a man in a pure, innocent, and sexless way. In short, she was about to embark on a brand new love affair of an entirely different nature.

"You can't wait to see him again, can you?" Vienna said.

"He said he's looking forward to it."

"Maybe he'll kiss you again, Jules."

"Maybe he'll kiss you, too."

Vienna nodded. "I'm glad you finally have the father you've always wanted."

"He's your father, too."

"But I think you always needed him more than I did," Vienna remarked.

Juliet thought about this for a minute. "He really is ours, isn't he?"

"Yes, he is."

Juliet wagged her head. "Just seems so unreal."

"Tell me about it."

Juliet looked at the wooden clock on the mantel. It was twenty minutes to seven.

"I guess we should head over to Cassandra's," she said.

Vienna nodded.

"She's not going to school on Monday, is she?" Juliet asked.

"Tomorrow's Monday."

"Oh, that's right." Juliet sighed and rubbed her temples. "I just can't keep track of time anymore." She sighed. "That poor girl. She wanted so much for Maxi to see her get into medical school one day. Make him proud."

"I know."

"Vien, maybe she should sleep here tonight instead."

"Yeah, that might be a better idea. We'll see what she wants to do." Vienna looked at Juliet. "That might work out better for you, too. Staying overnight in Maxi's house, surrounded by photos of him—"

"I can handle it. When's the funeral?"

"Tuesday morning," Vienna said. "Romy made the arrangements."

"Okay."

"Jules, for what it's worth, I'm glad I turned out to be wrong about Maxi raping Mom."

"Yeah, who would have thought the search for the mysterious rapist would have ended this way? Instead of finding a rapist, we found our father."

Vienna nodded. "Pleasant surprise, to say the least."

That was Juliet's only consolation after losing Maxi.

CHAPTER TWENTY

"Cassandra?"

Vienna rang Maxi's doorbell four or five times but got no response. She banged the brass, lion's-head doorknocker and called out Cassandra's name again.

"Maybe she's upstairs sleeping," Juliet said. "Try the door."

Vienna turned the knob. The door opened. She and Juliet stepped inside and closed the door. The blue sofa pillows were strewn on the beige carpet. The telephone had been disconnected and pushed off the wooden end table by the blue leather sofa. Pewter-framed photos of Maxi's late wife and Cassandra had been knocked off the mantel, and the glass was broken. Big shards of blue porcelain from a lamp were scattered across the carpet, and the shade had become detached from it and was lying lopsided on the carpet a couple of feet away.

"Cass, where are you?" Vienna shouted. "Are you all right?"

Juliet tugged on her arm and pointed to a zig-zag of crimson splotches on the carpet. They came from the kitchen and led to the living room closet. Vienna crept up to the closet and put her hand on the doorknob.

"Wait." Juliet was taking heavy, quivering breaths now. "I can't look at this." Then she realized that if Cassandra was in there, she could still be alive. "All right, go ahead. Open it."

Vienna slowly turned the knob. It squeaked a bit. She opened the door. Cassandra's mutilated body had been stuffed behind the rack of jackets and coats. She looked like she'd been stabbed in the chest multiple times. Juliet's mouth dropped open. Tears immediately filled her eyes. Finding Cassandra like that was horrible enough.

She hadn't expected to find Victor's body there, too.

"Oh, my God." Vienna's voice was hushed and shaky.

"Miranda's targeting everyone who knew Maxi." Juliet felt Victor's wrist and then Cassandra's. She sighed and shook her head. It was too late.

Victor's newfound role in her life had been too good to be true, just like her blossoming romance with Maxi. Twice she had lost Victor, but this time she could see with her own eyes that he was gone for good. Within twenty-four hours, she'd lost the two most important men in her life. She held Victor's hand in both of hers, wanting and needing to feel connected to him one last time. His hand was still warm. She pressed the back of it against her teary cheek.

"I don't get this," Vienna said. "Victor didn't know Maxi."

"Yes, he did. He told me that he met Maxi once. Romy introduced them."

"How did Miranda know that?" Vienna asked.

"Maybe she was watching somewhere in the distance when it happened. I don't know how she got to Victor in the first place. When he left me at St. Anthony's, he was probably headed for the rectory. Maybe she snuck in there somehow. I guess she brought his body here to slight Maxi's memory, since it's his house." She rubbed her temples as she felt a serious headache coming on. "Vien, I didn't know how to tell you this before. Miranda drove by our house yesterday. She saw me on the front porch, kissing Maxi goodbye."

"She knows where we live? Oh, great! *Now* what the hell are we gonna do?"

"We've got to find Romy," Juliet said.

"That's right, Miranda might be at her place right now. We've got to get over there."

"Romy's not there."

The twins looked up the stairs, in the direction where they'd heard the voice. A sandy-blond young man was coming down the stairs, his faded jeans and grey T-shirt stained with blood.

"So that girl in the closet was actually telling the truth when she said she was expecting two girlfriends. Like she thought that was supposed to scare me off." He laughed like an obnoxious drunk. "Stupid bitch. But I've got to hand it to her. She did put up a damn good fight, clobbering me over the head with the lamp and those pictures."

"You killed both these people?" Juliet demanded.

"Yeah, I did," he said, getting in her face. "You got a problem with that?"

"What did you do to Romy?" Vienna asked.

"Nothing. I went to her house, but she wasn't home. I told you that already."

"What were you doing upstairs?"

"Looking for valuable jewelry," he said, "but there isn't any."

"Who are you?" Juliet asked.

"Remington Key. Call me Remmy."

Suddenly Juliet's blood went cold as she took a closer look at this beast of a person and noticed his violet-blue eyes.

"Are you Miranda Key's brother?" she asked.

"No. Miranda doesn't have a brother. I'm her son."

"Wait, you're the kid she got knocked up with when she was sixteen?" Vienna asked.

"Yeah, that's right."

"Why the hell did you kill our father and our best friend?" Vienna snapped.

"Who?"

"The two people in the closet," Juliet said.

"So you'll get a new pastor. Big deal."

"He wasn't our priest," Vienna said. "That's not the kind of father I'm talking about."

Remmy scrunched up his eyebrows. "You mean your dad was a *priest?*"

"That's right."

He looked like he'd just found dead flies floating in his cereal bowl. "That is so perverted!"

"Why would you kill a priest?"

"He knew Maxi," Remmy said. "I saw him talking to Romy and Maxi once."

"How do you even know what Romy and Maxi look like?" Juliet asked.

"I saw their pictures in the yearbook. That priest was friends with Romy, and Romy was friends with Maxi, and Maxi made my mom's life a living hell back in high school. And that's why I killed the priest. It's called guilt by association. I spotted him coming out of church and walking across the street to the rectory, and bam! I ran him the hell down. And it was no problem picking up his body and putting him in the car, because nobody was around to see me do it. This Tiger Lily is even deader than a cemetery. How can you stand living here?"

"You killed Maxi, didn't you?" Juliet said. "*You* ran him down last night."

"Yeah, I did. What's it to you?"

"He was my boyfriend!"

"Did you rape our friend in there?" Vienna asked, pointing to the closet.

"No, I don't rape brunettes."

"What's that supposed to mean?" Juliet asked. "You rape blonds?"

"I didn't say that."

Vienna eyed him suspiciously and shook her head. "You know, a shrink could have a lot of fun trying to figure out just what the hell's your problem. I mean, if you really think about it, the possibilities seem endless! On the surface, it seems like this is all about a boy who's trying to protect his mama from the big, bad wolf Maxi who supposedly ruined her life. But who knows? Maybe you're pissed off because you don't have a dad, so you want to take everyone else's dad away from them. Maybe you're pissed off because you're an only child, and you resent the fact that my sister and I have each other."

"Maxi was an only child," Juliet murmured sadly, half to herself.

"Maybe you hate priests because they represent God, and you don't believe in God because you had an unhappy childhood. Maybe you kill young women because deep down you resent your mom for not telling you who your dad is. Or perhaps you just can't stand to accept the truth about your mom—that she was a teenage tramp, and she doesn't even *know* who your dad is."

"Vienna." Juliet made a slashing motion across her neck.

"That's all right, let her finish," Remmy said.

Vienna continued. "Maybe you're angry because you think you *do* have a half-brother or sister out there somewhere. Maybe your father got married and had a family. Who knows? And you're mad as hell because you know you'll never be able to track down that sibling, because your mom doesn't know who your dad is. See, it all comes back to your mom. She's the cause of all your misery, not Maxi. Why can't you admit that she's the one you really hate?"

Remmy sat surprisingly calm and relaxed in his chair, his body shifted to one side and his legs crossed. He scratched his chin thoughtfully.

"You going to college?" he asked.

"Yes."

"Where?"

"Columbia," she said.

"Is that the kind of psychoanalytical crap they're teaching you big-shot Ivy League chicks?"

"Listen to me, you damn well better be telling the truth about Romy not being home," Vienna said. "Because so help me, if you killed her, too—"

"She's not home. Why would I lie about that?"

"We were told that your mother is a perpetual liar," Juliet said. "Maybe you take after her."

He grabbed her by the throat and shook her hard. "Enough about my mother!"

Vienna picked up a shard of porcelain on the floor, and she scraped it across his arm, drawing blood. He screamed and let go of Juliet's throat, breaking off the heart locket in the process. Juliet tried to pull it out of his fingers, but he pushed her away and opened the locket.

"Maxi Ward. Who else?" He turned it over. "Aw, ain't that sweet. The son of a bitch loves you—or he did anyway." He rubbed the engraved side against the cherry coffee table, making disturbing scratching noises like someone running their fingernails across a blackboard. He removed the photo and ripped it into tiny pieces, then he broke the two sides of the heart from the hinges and handed the entire mess to Juliet with an impish smile. "There you go."

She sat in silence as she stared at the broken clasp of the gold chain, the broken pieces of the heart locket, and Maxi's damaged face.

"The clasp can be fixed, Jules," Vienna said, putting an arm around her.

But of the three precious things that Remmy had damaged, the chain and the locket meant the least to her. It was at that moment that a horrible realization crept into her mind, something she hadn't noticed when she first walked into Maxi's trashed living room. She sprung to her feet and hustled over to the shattered photos of Maxi's family, which were lying on the floor near the fireplace. Juliet crouched on the carpet and frantically shuffled through the photos but found that Maxi's face had been torn out of all of them.

She headed toward the stairs in a frenzy, praying that there were other photos of him in his bedroom. That was probably where he'd kept his yearbooks and his wedding album.

"Don't bother," Remmy said. "There's nothing up there."

She stopped in her tracks. "What did you do with Maxi's pictures?"

"I tore them all up and flushed them down the toilet," he said.

"Why?"

"Because I couldn't flush Maxi himself down the toilet, and that was the next best thing."

Juliet felt her heart shrivel up inside her chest. Never again would Maxi's beautiful dark eyes gaze at her, not even in a photograph. As she sadly turned away from the stairs, something pink caught her eye inside the desk against the living room wall. The drawer had been left partially open. Maybe Cassandra had frantically searched in there for a sharp object to fend off Remmy with, and she left the drawer that way. Juliet opened the drawer all the way and took out the pink item. It was the size of a jewelry box, wrapped in baby pink paper and a pink lace ribbon. Her heart started to race, because she already knew what was inside. With trembling hands, she slowly untied the ribbon and removed the wrapping. She opened the black velvet box. Inside it was a heart pendant that was twice the size of the yellow gold heart locket she'd worn for years. The new pendant was a rose gold puffed heart. Nestled inside the box was a note that read:

> "Juliet,
> This one is puffed because my heart is swelled with love for only you, baby girl.
>
> Love, Maxi"

She turned the heart over. On the back were these words:

> "Marry me."

Her lower lip quaked. Now her heart was shriveling up so much that she barely even realized she was still alive. She closed her eyes and slowly raked her fingers over her face, dropping the pendant on the floor. Two days ago she was happier than she'd ever been, and now the tears that she couldn't shed before had finally arrived, in full force. She would have had everything she always wanted—a future with Maxi and a relationship with her father. She and Maxi would have had children together. She would have known the pleasures of having all those perks that Maxi's late wife had in all the years she was married to him. And best of all, the two most important men in Juliet's life would have had the chance to know each other.

But Remmy took it all away.

"Stop that crying!" he yelled.

"Leave her alone," Vienna said. "She hasn't been able to cry for him until now. She's been in shock."

"Who cares? I can't stand that sobbing. The last time I got laid, the damn redhead freaked me out and started up just like that. She had some weird name. What the hell was it? Something with 'city.' Felicity!"

Vienna's silver-blue eyes widened as though she'd just seen a dead person come back to life and crawl out of his grave.

"Felicity?"

"Yeah, that's right," he said.

Juliet swallowed. She suddenly realized that she had stopped crying, and now her eyes were ping-ponging back and forth between Vienna and Remmy.

"What was her last name?" Vienna asked. "How old was she?"

"I don't know. Maybe late thirties."

Vienna kneed him in the genitals. He doubled over, the air whooshing right out of his lungs.

"What was her last name, man?" she hollered.

"That was it!" He was straining his voice as he remained on his knees, clutching his crotch. "Felicity Mann."

"Did you rape her?"

He nodded slowly. "I rang her doorbell. Pulled the old 'car broke down and I need to use the phone' trick, and she fell for it and let me in." He laughed. "Works every time."

Vienna snatched the large Austrian crystal bowl from the center of the coffee table and slugged him sideways in the head with it, slicing the air so frighteningly fast that Juliet barely saw what had happened.

"She was our mother!" Vienna cried.

Juliet grabbed Vienna's arm to stop her, but Vienna pushed her away and swung the bowl at him again and again, splattering blood on the wall behind him.

"My God, Vien, what the hell are you doing?" Juliet cried.

He pouted his lower lip and wept silently as he writhed in pain. His face looked like a piece of raw, bloody meat. His head was bobbing a little. Juliet could see that he was half-dead already. Blood was streaming down his face and the sides of his head, soaking his sandy blond hair. He had a shameful look on his face, like a teenager who'd just wrecked the family car and was about to suffer his parents' wrath. His violet-blue eyes looked like a bottomless black pit. The sad little boy with the mama fixation was devoid of words. All he ever wanted to be was his mother's hero, Remington the protector and savior. He needed her to need him.

He needed *someone* to need him.

Then again, maybe Vienna was right. Maybe he was furious at his mother and was inflicting his anger on the rest of the world. Whatever the truth, it was going to die with him. Suddenly it occurred to Juliet that this was the case in all aspects of life, with everyone and everything. She was never going to solve the mystery of the sadness in Maxi's eyes. She was never going to learn what part of his checkered past he seemed so reluctant to share with her, or what had inspired him to become a teacher. Never was she going to find out how or when Cassandra's feelings of friendship for Vienna had deepened into love. She and Vienna were never going to understand why Felicity didn't report the rape to the police and punish Remmy, rather than take her own life and punish herself.

Some things were just meant to remain mysterious, for no particular reason—and that in and of itself was a mystery.

Vienna grabbed the coffee table by the legs and threw it on top of Remmy. It met his body with an abrasive thud, and suddenly the moaning stopped.

"What the hell is wrong with you, Vien?"

"You wanted him dead, too," Vienna said, staggering around the room like a drunk and trying to catch her breath. "But you weren't going to do it, because you don't have it in you."

Juliet pushed the coffee table off of Remmy, sending it crashing to the floor. She felt his neck, then she stood up and planted her hands on her hips. "I don't know how to reach you anymore, Vien. You're too far gone!"

"Relax, he's not dead. He's faking it, just like the killers in the horror movies. He's playing games with us, trying to make our life even more of a living hell than it already is."

"You know, Vien, I like to tell myself that temporary insanity makes you do the crazy things you do. But it can't be temporary insanity, because you do so many of them!"

"Didn't I tell you Mom was raped?"

"Yes, you did," Juliet said, "and I didn't want to believe you at first."

"I said don't get involved with Maxi. Something horrendous is going to come of it. You didn't want to believe that either!"

"Well, how was I supposed to know that Miranda's kid was a psycho who wanted to slice and dice everyone who knew Maxi? And all because of some stupid joke that Maxi told about her way back in high school?"

"Hell, maybe the broad really *was* a hooker and a porno queen," Vienna said. "What do we know?"

"It's all over, Vien. That's what we know. You've pissed it all away!"

"Take it easy, Jules."

"You don't get it, do you? This isn't like what you did to Maxi, punching him out at the cemetery. It isn't like what you did to Kelly Kline and Richard on the high school football field. This one's not coming back!"

"Oh, he'll come back. They all come back." There was a hint of tears in Vienna's voice. "Bad guys never die."

"This one did." Juliet felt his neck again to be sure.

"You know, I *thought* there was something screwy about Romy's story—Mom killing herself over a man. How many women really do that?"

"So Romy didn't know about the rape?"

"I guess not," Vienna said. "Maybe she just assumed that Victor was the reason for the suicide. Apparently Mom *didn't* confide in Romy about everything."

The girls jumped at the sound of the doorbell. Vienna stood on her toes and peered through the glass above the front door.

"Who is it, Vien?"

"Some hot looking Sharon Stone type with eyes like Liz Taylor."

CHAPTER TWENTY-ONE

"Juliet?" the woman asked.

"No, I'm Vienna, Jules' twin sister."

"Hello, I'm Miranda Key. Is my son Remington here?"

"He sure is." Vienna held the door open. "Come on in."

Juliet suddenly felt weak and faint. What the hell was Vienna thinking?

Miranda sashayed into the living room in that sexy, sassy way of hers. The sight of Remmy's crumpled, bloody remains on the floor put an abrupt end to that wanton walk. She screamed and knelt over him, feeling his neck for a pulse, then she hung her head and sobbed. As she kissed him goodbye on his forehead, the ends of her perfectly coifed blond hair became tinged with his blood and stained her white dress.

"Who did this?" she asked.

"I did," Vienna said, remaining unbelievably calm and composed.

Miranda looked at her with piercing eyes as she stood up. "Why did you kill my son?"

"Why are you even here?"

"Remmy called me and asked me to come over," Miranda said. "He said he wanted to show me something."

"Oh, my God. He wanted to show off what he did. Make Mommy proud. That's like a cat killing a mouse and showing it to his owner!"

"What are you talking about?" Miranda asked.

Vienna motioned with her head toward the closet. "Take a look at your son's handiwork."

Miranda peered in the closet and immediately backed away, turning back to the twins with a nauseous look on her face.

"How do you know Remmy did this?" she asked.

"He told us," Juliet said. "He said he killed Maxi, too."

"Who's the girl?"

"Maxi's daughter," Vienna said.

"Thank God he didn't rape her." Miranda paused, then she added under her breath, "He only attacked redheads."

"Redheads!" Vienna grabbed her by the throat and shoved her against the wall. "You know he raped our mother, and you helped him cover it up!"

"What the hell are you talking about?"

"Our mother was a redhead," Vienna said. "You said he only attacked redheads."

"No, I didn't," Miranda stammered. "I said he was only *attracted* to redheads."

"You said he only attacked redheads," Juliet said. "If you mean attacked as in 'raped,' then please tell us, who else did he rape?"

"I didn't say he raped anyone."

"But you know that he raped our mother, don't you?" Juliet said. "Felicity Mann. You went to high school with her."

"He raped Felicity? I heard she committed suicide a few weeks ago."

"She did, because your son raped her!"

Miranda's eyes looked startled, sad, and faraway all at once. "Oh, my God, that's nine," she mumbled to herself.

"Nine victims?" Vienna shoved her harder against the wall. "Damn you, woman, what the hell kind of twisted bastard did you raise?"

"Don't call him that!" Miranda pushed Vienna off of her.

"You know what I mean. Look, whatever Remmy did, just say it. Don't lie and don't play dumb. It won't do you any good, because Jules and I are on to you now. Romy clued us in."

"You know Romaine?"

"Like a second mother," Juliet said. "She helped our mom raise us."

"We know about the bogus rape charge," Vienna said. "We know you scared the hell out of Romy with that threatening look in the girls' bathroom so she wouldn't testify against you."

"All right, I get it," Miranda said. "You're Romy's friend and now it's payback time." She lowered her head shamefully. "When Remmy was in high school and college, eight girls—all redheads—accused him of rape. They all pressed charges against him. But right before their trials were set to begin, the girls were murdered. Some were stabbed, and the others were run down. The police never caught the killer." The twins looked at Miranda suspiciously. "Look, even if I did know for a fact that he killed them, I would have done anything to keep my son out of prison."

"So he'd be free to kill again and rape our mother?" Vienna said.

"I swear I didn't know about that," Miranda insisted, holding up her right hand. "I never mentioned Felicity's name to him. Maybe he went to the high school library and flipped through my yearbook—I mean what *would* have been my yearbook if I'd graduated. Maybe he wanted to see what my classmates looked like, and that was when he saw her picture. He knew she was a redhead, because the yearbook is in color. He must have found her address in the phone book."

"You don't know the hell our mother was going through before Remmy came along," Juliet said. "She was already depressed about losing our father. He wouldn't leave the priesthood for her and for us. Your son added to her anguish by raping her. He drove her over the edge."

A shadow of bewilderment fell upon Miranda's face. "Is that priest in the closet your father?"

"Yes," Vienna said. "And the girl was our best friend and the only person who ever had romantic feelings for me. I didn't love her in that way, but still it was nice to know that someone cared—even though I didn't appreciate it at the time. Your son took all that away. He took *everything* away, and that's why I killed him!"

"Wait a minute," Miranda said. "Are you saying that Felicity Mann slept with a priest?" She shook her head. "No way, you can't be talking about the same Felicity Mann I knew."

Vienna nodded. "Blows your mind, doesn't it?"

"But she and Romy were the two most virginal girls in school!"

"Maybe Romy was, but our mother wasn't," Vienna said.

"How old was this priest when she allegedly slept with him?"

"Twenty-nine," Vienna said.

Miranda gasped. "Felicity Mann slept with a twenty-nine-year-old man when she was a teenager?" She snickered. "That alone is shocking, and on top of that the man was a priest? Even I didn't get lucky with men that age when I was in high school. Who told you this?"

"Romy did, just last night."

Suddenly it was as though the proverbial light bulb glowed in Miranda's face. "Oh, my God, I always knew those two were keeping secrets, but I never thought they were anything like this!"

Vienna glared at her. "Felicity Mann and Romaine Confidelle are the two finest women Jules and I have ever known, regardless of the secret they kept."

"Confidelle?" Miranda looked puzzled. "That's not Romy's last name."

"Yes, it is."

"Not back in high school, it wasn't," Miranda said. "It was Desiderio."

Vienna laughed uncontrollably, bending over and slapping her thigh. "Desiderio!" Her eyes became watery. "Thanks a lot, Miranda. I needed a good laugh."

Miranda gave her a sour look. "What is so funny?"

"Desiderio was our father's name," Juliet explained.

"So Romy must be related to him somehow," Miranda said.

Vienna stopped laughing. Her silver-blue eyes turned steely.

"Romy is related to us, and she's been keeping it a secret for the past twenty years?"

"Apparently," Miranda said.

Vienna looked at Miranda as though the Sharon Stone look-alike were the devil incarnate.

"Romy warned us about you," Vienna said. "She told us never to believe anything you say."

"She would never keep that from us all our lives," Juliet said.

"Why not?" Miranda said. "She waited all this time to tell you the truth about your father."

"But that was the only secret," Vienna said. "She said there were no more, and I believe her."

"You shouldn't," Miranda said. "There's another one out there. There's *always* another one with Romy. You don't know her as well as you think you do."

"We've known her for twenty years!"

"Yeah, but I know the *real* Romy, from way back when she was just a kid," Miranda said. "Tell me something, is she married? Is she seeing anyone?"

"No. Why?"

"She doesn't need a man in her life," Miranda said. "She has her secrets to sustain her. She's married to them! Don't you see? I didn't want you to find out the secret she knew about me. She doesn't want you to find out the secret I know about *her.* That's why she told you not to listen to me. Look, it seems you girls have been kept in the dark way too long. I'm just trying to help you."

"You didn't help us before," Juliet said. "You lied to me about Maxi raping you, and I was stupid enough to believe you at first. I won't make that mistake again. You knew Romy was Maxi's friend, and you held it against her. That's why you're lying about her now."

"I had nothing against Romy. It's just that she had this spooky alliance with Felicity. I used to see them in the hallway, whispering and looking over their shoulders like they were keeping dreadful secrets from the rest of the world." Miranda let out a short laugh. "And you say Romy is afraid of me? She's scarier than I am, in her own quiet way. I'm afraid of *her!*"

Vienna looked frustrated, like a caged tiger in a zoo, and suddenly Juliet began to grow fearful. The whirlwind of torment that had been swallowing up Vienna these past few weeks was now spiraling out of control.

"Felicity and Romy really did a job on you girls, didn't they?" Miranda said. "All these years they were keeping secrets that even I wouldn't have kept from my own flesh and blood. But I've got to hand it to them, in a way. I never would have thought those two wallflowers had it in them to pull off something like this. What a hypocrite Romy is, miss holier-than-thou."

Vienna's right arm shot out, and her fist met Miranda's nose. Miranda staggered backward, yelping in pain and grabbing her bloody nose.

"Don't listen to her, Vien," Juliet said, pulling her away from Miranda. "She's just getting back at you for killing her son." She eyed Miranda coldly. "Because of your lies, I fought with Maxi the night before he died. Thank God we made up, but if it hadn't been for that lie, I never would have fought with him in the first place."

"All right, I admit that I lied about Maxi raping me. But I swear I'm not lying about Romy's real name. She hasn't always been honest with you either. Why do you believe *her*?"

"Because we know her," Vienna said. "We don't know you, and we don't *want* to know you. Who are you anyway? You come blowing into our lives like a damn hurricane, and all of a sudden Jules and I find ourselves being attacked by all the terrible T words: tragedy, treachery, trickery, torture, torment, terror, trouble, tension, trepidation, and God knows what else. And it's all because of some dopey, locker-room joke that you got overly sensitive about in high school. Why couldn't you just say, 'The hell with Maxi' and get on with your life?"

"That joke ruined the rest of my time in school," Miranda said. "Everyone took it seriously. Every time my teachers looked at me, I thought they were going to vomit. My grades went down the toilet. My guidance counselor dragged me into her office at least once a week to interrogate me about my sexual habits. My parents forced me to see a therapist for people with a sexual compulsive problem. When I refused to go, they threw me out of the house and wouldn't let me back in until I said I'd go. I had to spend a few nights on the street, where I almost *did* get raped. And all because Maxi, may he rot in hell, told a joke that I was a hooker and a porno queen."

"Why didn't you stay at a friend's house when your parents threw you out?" Vienna asked.

"None of my friends' parents would let me."

"Maxi doesn't deserve to rot in hell," Juliet said to Miranda. "Damn you for hoping he does!"

"Trust me, honey, you didn't even know him." Miranda turned to Vienna. "Nobody ever did," she added eerily.

"I knew him much better than you did," Juliet said. "You knew Maxi the teenager. I knew Maxi the man. We would have gotten married if your son hadn't killed him."

"Then consider yourself lucky. Remmy saved you from yourself. He did you a favor."

Juliet gasped. "Remmy was the rapist, not Maxi, and you have the nerve to praise Remmy and badmouth Maxi?" She whacked Miranda hard across the face.

Miranda looked at her through narrowed eyes as she rubbed her cheek. "If you're so certain that Maxi loved you, then why were you jealous of me when I told you about me and Maxi at that party together?"

"What are you talking about?"

"You felt threatened by me, Jule. I picked up on that. You thought I was going to lure Maxi away from you." Miranda's mouth formed an icy, wicked smile. "And you know what?" She moved her face closer to Juliet's and whispered, "If I really wanted to, I could have—like *that*. Even though I pressed charges against him years ago, he would have been thrilled to have me again. Because when all was said and done, Maxi Ward was all about sex. And, honey, no woman in Tiger Lily is more learned on that subject than I am."

Juliet stood firm before her. She refused to let Miranda taunt her, distort Maxi's memory, and sabotage her belief in the love that she and Maxi had shared.

"I know Maxi was an extremely sexual man, Miranda. He was a Scorpio! But he didn't want *you* anymore. He said you left him unsatisfied. You teased him, tantalized him, and sexually frustrated the hell out of him!"

"So what? He enjoyed it. By the time I got finished with him, he was salivating all over the damn place. Every time I think about those revolting rumors he spread, I want to bring him back to life and frustrate him all over again. I'm a lot older and wiser now. I could make it ten times worse and plague him with all kinds of sexual itches that he never even knew existed. Then I'd steal away and leave him ungratified yet again." She threw back her head and laughed haughtily. "Ah well, maybe I'll see him in my dreams some night. And if I do, Juliet, I'll tell your lover man that you said hello, and I'll send him your love—while I'm sexually frustrating the hell out of him."

"You take enormous pleasure in being a bitch, don't you?" Vienna said. "You waltz in here, you try to make my sister feel insecure about her relationship with her dead lover, and you fill our heads with lies about Romy being related to us. What the hell's next?"

"You love Romy," Miranda said. "Don't you *want* to be related to her?"

"Of course we do. That's the point. Romy knows that Jules and I love her, and we know she loves us. So if she were related to us, why would she keep it a secret?"

"Maybe she's ashamed of you," Miranda said. "Can you blame her?

Look at you two. You're a mess! Romy knows that. She doesn't want to get swallowed up in the kooky, obsessive-compulsive world you girls live in with your freaky conglomeration of family and friends. Jule, you loved Maxi even though he used to hit your mother. And, Vienna, his daughter loved you even though you hated her father. Your father, a priest, took a teenage girl to bed and committed statutory rape. He made her fall in love with him, he seduced her and got her pregnant, and then he left her high and dry. You people are the saddest, sorriest, scariest damn bunch of dysfunctional human beings I've ever known!"

"I can't believe what I'm hearing," Vienna said. "Your deranged son wiped out almost every person we loved, and you have the audacity to stand there and call *us* dysfunctional?"

"That's right. No wonder Romy's keeping her mouth shut. Hell, if I were related to a pitiful, romantic fool and her hot-headed psychopath twin, I wouldn't be all fired up to announce it to the world either. Wake up, girls! Romy doesn't love you. She just feels sorry for you. She thinks of you as her own personal, twenty-year-long charity case."

Vienna lunged at Miranda and socked her in the face, sending her toppling to the floor, where Vienna continued to pummel her like a heavyweight in the ring. Juliet pressed her long fingernails into the back of Vienna's neck. Vienna shrieked and flinched, stumbling away from Miranda and rubbing her neck. Juliet pushed Vienna away from Miranda. Vienna grabbed the disconnected phone that had been knocked to the floor and hurled it at Miranda's head but missed it by a hair.

"Stop it!" Juliet cried, grabbing Vienna's arm.

"Bastards, bitches, and liars," Vienna mumbled. "Murderers and rapists. That's all we see anymore, Jules. I get rid of one, and another one shows up." She clung to Juliet and buried her face in Juliet's shoulder, as though seeking some kind of solace and escape from the villain-infested world. "It never ends."

Her sobs were long and ragged, like Juliet's own sobs at Felicity's funeral and probably like the horrific sobs that Felicity had uttered when Remmy raped her. But Vienna's sobs conveyed so much more than sorrow or shame. They told Juliet that Vienna had no more fight left in her.

Juliet's head felt like a washing machine, but a myriad of emotions took the place of clothes tumbling around madly. She was furious at Remington and Miranda, all the while mourning the loss of her loved ones and worrying whether she and Romy would be able to pull Vienna out of the dark pit that she kept falling deeper and deeper into. They were going to have to find a damn good lawyer to defend her, a magic man who could pull rabbits out of a hat. That was what it was going to take to get Vienna out of this mess. So Juliet decided that it was best to save her own tears for later. Right now she needed to be strong for Vienna, the only living relative she had left. This was a weird, scary feeling indeed. For years, she'd been accustomed to Vienna's overprotective nature. Now it was her turn to protect Vienna.

Vienna let go of her and wiped her tears. "I need some water."

A shaky Miranda zipped open her white eelskin purse, pulled out a pack of tissues, and wiped off the blood around her nose and mouth. The skin around her right eye looked like the color of the sky just before a rainstorm. She stood up unsteadily as Vienna disappeared into the kitchen. Miranda pulled a black cell phone out of her purse, but Juliet yanked it out of her hand. She held the phone in the air, wanting to strike Miranda with it, realizing that this must have been what it felt like to live inside of Vienna's skin. On that note, Juliet managed to find her sanity again, realizing that *someone* in that house had to keep her temper in check.

"You venomous, black-hearted bitch! Listen, my sister may be violent, but she's extremely bright. She's been pulling a 4.0 at Columbia every semester for the past three years. Romy is *not* ashamed of her. She's very proud of her, and she does love her. You think I'm jealous of you? You're the one who's jealous, of me and Vienna. We have a wonderful friend who loves us. The only person who loved *you* was a serial rapist and murderer! I shouldn't have interfered when Vienna tried to kill you. I'd love to kill you myself!"

"Go ahead, I don't care anymore. My son is gone. My life is over." Miranda's voice was muffled with tears. "I wanted him to turn out better than I did. I'm sorry I didn't do a better job raising him. I'm sorry I'm never going to have the chance to tell him that."

Juliet felt just a shred of empathy for this emotionally fractured woman. Maybe Miranda would have made a good wife if the right man had come along, a man who would have looked beyond the beautiful face. She'd been disgusted, perhaps, and had given up hope.

Maybe she'd turned bitter and cold and settled for sex, because in her mind it was the next best thing. Maybe she'd never figured out how to relate to men on a deeper level. After all, sex was much easier for a girl to get than love. Practically all she had to do was snap her fingers and it would come running, like people would do if they saw someone throw bundles of cash into the street.

Juliet headed for the kitchen to see whether Vienna had calmed down. Suddenly her heart sank down to her gut. She dropped Miranda's cell phone on the sofa. Through the doorway of the kitchen, Juliet saw a streak of red liquid spreading across the white tiles of the kitchen floor. She rushed into the room. Vienna was lying on her back. A steak knife was sticking out of her chest, and blood was dripping down her motionless body. Juliet screamed Vienna's name as she felt her neck for a pulse. Nothing. No, that couldn't be right. Juliet felt Vienna's wrist. Still nothing. She desperately checked her neck again. Maybe she was doing it wrong. But she'd done it the same way when she checked Remmy's pulse. Juliet closed her eyes for a minute, wishfully thinking that when she opened them, Vienna would be stirring.

Juliet mentally rewound the last five minutes. She shouldn't have let Vienna go into the kitchen alone. She should have known what would happen. As she cradled Vienna in her arms and cried into her hair, she thought about the trip that they were never going to take.

"I'm sorry, Juliet," Miranda said, bending over and touching her arm.

"Get away from her!" Juliet cried, holding Vienna protectively. "Everything you touch winds up dead." She laid Vienna on the floor and stumbled into the living room again. Suddenly the air got thicker, and she felt like she could barely breathe. "I've got to get out of here."

She headed for the door, but Miranda grabbed her arm. "Wait, you can't leave."

After trying unsuccessfully to shake her arm free, Juliet grabbed the cell phone on the sofa and walloped Miranda across the face with it, sending her stumbling across the room where she hit her head against the corner of the coffee table. Juliet ran out the door, dying to get out of the stifling confines of the house and into the fresh air.

The minute she stepped off the front porch, she remained with her mouth open. For a few seconds, she wondered whether she was actually seeing what she thought she was seeing or whether she was imagining it to help take her mind off of all the violence she'd witnessed.

"Oh, my God," she murmured.

Flashes of flaming red and opalescent pink were streaked across the mellow blue sky. A couple of seconds later, the pink turned into lavender and the baby blue deepened into periwinkle. It was now eight o'clock in the evening, and the sun was starting to go down. Soon she would be enveloped by darkness, that mystical thing that Maxi found so soothing and life-affirming. From now on, whenever it turned dark, she would think of Maxi. But for now, she wanted to revel in the incredible beauty of the sky before darkness fell. She remembered Vienna mentioning once how gorgeous the sky was at this time of day, but Juliet had never bothered to look at it until now. Perhaps everyone else in Tiger Lily had seen and appreciated it before, too, to the point where it was no longer considered a wondrous spectacle. It was a common occurrence, so they took it for granted. But for Juliet, it was a personal awakening. It was almost as though the red of the sky symbolized blood, and the world was closing in on her, just like the walls of Maxi's house seemed to be doing a minute ago.

But at the same time she felt like the sky was reaching out and introducing itself to her. Mother Nature was saying hello through the fuchsia rhododendrons, smiley-faced yellow and purple pansies, and red hyacinths that decorated the lawns of Clover Lane. She was calling out to Juliet via the delicate mimosa on Romy's front lawn and through Charlotte Sloane's garden of violet-blue irises, white crocuses, and sherbet-colored tulips that were perked up high and straight like soldiers standing at attention. For years Vienna had admired and pointed out this lush garden to Juliet. But Juliet had always taken it for granted, because for four years her mind had been focused solely on Maxi, to the point where she couldn't even see what had been right in front of her. Now she realized that there was beauty in the world besides Maxi, and that the world was made up of so many other ordinary yet extraordinary things besides Maxi.

And maybe—just maybe—she could get by without Maxi. As a matter of fact, maybe this was his final gift to her. Perhaps he was using the vibrant colors of the sky as a way of communicating with her from the other side. She smiled up at the heavens.

"Maxi . . ." she whispered.

Now she realized why Dr. Thorne was always so cheerful during his morning jog. To live on a beautiful street like Clover Lane was an incredible privilege.

She wondered why she'd suddenly been hit with this appreciation for nature after so many years of indifference toward it. Her adrenaline must have been pumping because of the tragedies occurring all around her, which made her powers of observation keener and her senses more perceptive. She also wondered how it was possible that the world could look so beautiful when so many of her loved ones were gone. Everyone and everything was gone, it seemed. Butterscotch was nowhere in sight. No chipmunks were scurrying through the grass. No squirrels were spiraling up the trees. The only animals Juliet spotted were two sparrows flitting around in the marble bird bath in Charlotte's garden, poking their beaks in the water and splashing the droplets around to cool themselves off on this unusually hot evening. One sparrow took flight, then the other. The birds soared high into the depths of the red and purple sky, but the second one couldn't catch up to the first. Higher and higher they flew until their tiny brown bodies seemed to blend into the sky, almost becoming swallowed up in it.

Juliet thought about dear, sweet Victor—the second man in her life, the one who had lifted her up and brought her back to life after Maxi's death. She cried over the fact that she was only starting to get a taste of what it would have felt like to love him when he'd been so senselessly taken from her. But then she dried her tears when she realized how grateful she was for having met him and for the few precious memories he'd left her, even though their time together had been so painfully short. In her mind she relived that moment in the pew at St. Anthony's when he'd planted that gentle kiss on her cheek, the most beautiful kiss any man had ever given her. Suddenly she was feeling his warm hand on her face again. But this time she added something to that heartfelt scene. She imagined herself embracing him, like Vienna had said she should have done. She closed her eyes and stretched out her arms.

"Victor," she would have called out softly as he was leaving the pew.

He turned to face her again. She wrapped her arms around his shoulders. He slid his arms around her waist. She pressed him close to her and rested her cheek on his shoulder. He was never going to leave her again. Everything was going to be different now. They were going to have the rest of their lives together. She smiled softly as she held the moment in her mind. She didn't want it to end, because if it did, then he would be gone. It would almost be like losing him all over again, for the third time.

Then the image was broken as the tips of Juliet's toes suddenly rammed against what felt like an uneven sidewalk, and she was thrust onto the ground with a force so strong that her entire body hit the pavement and rolled fast and hard until the side of her head hit a telephone pole.

And then the vision of Victor was gone and everything else right along with it.

CHAPTER TWENTY-TWO

Father Sullivan slid open the screened panel in the confessional.

"Bless me, Father, for I have sinned," Romy whispered. "It's been two months since my last confession."

"What sins do you have to confess?"

Romy breathed shakily as she gathered her thoughts. "A secret, Father—one that I kept from my two nieces. They're both gone now. They died a couple of weeks ago. I kept this secret from them, because I was trying to protect someone else—my brother. He died on the same day. A lot of people died that day. I'm the one who found them all." She closed her eyes and shook her head, trying to erase the bloody memory of it. "One of the people was a woman I went to high school with, someone who I used to despise. But I suppose it would be hypocritical for me to judge Miranda harshly now, after what *I* did. As I said, I kept my nieces in the dark, never revealing my true identity to them. Their mother and I had agreed that if we told the girls the truth years ago, it only would have created complications for our family, especially for my brother and his professional welfare. The girls would have raised questions about their father that I wasn't prepared to answer. I wanted to do whatever I could to help him hold on to the career he'd worked so hard to maintain. So I thought that the less my nieces knew about him, the better. Had they lived, I *might* have told them everything months from now, after they'd recovered from the other recent shocks and tragedies in their lives. But now I'll never have the chance."

Romy reflected on the past couple of conversations she'd had with Juliet and Vienna, and suddenly everything made sense. No wonder Tiger Lily had been so dead these past three weeks, since Felicity's suicide. That deadness was an eerie foreshadowing that Felicity's death would not be the last. That was why Vienna had experienced that unshakable premonition that a catastrophe was about to wreck all of their lives. Tears welled up in Romy's eyes as she thought about it. No wonder Vienna thanked her for all that she'd done over the years. She probably sensed deep down, even then, that she was going to end her own life. And no wonder Juliet said that Maxi was the only man she was ever going to love.

But she probably had no idea just how right she was about that.

"I realize now," Romy said, "that I should have told them my secret when my niece Vienna asked me if there were any secrets left to tell. I know if I had, then she never would have taken her own life." She sighed. "She wanted to know whether there was something worth living for. I knew, but I didn't tell her." She shook her head sadly. "They were lost, both of them. They were two lonely, misguided girls with extremely fragile hearts. I knew this, but I should have known *better*. I should have been there for them, in a better way than I was. I took their pain for granted. If only I'd told them everything." She buried her face in her hands and wept. "But I couldn't bring myself to tell them anything, not even how much I loved them—especially my beautiful Vienna. And now I've lost them both."

She couldn't stop crying, and over and over she heard herself say the same thing because her despair kept her from knowing what else to say or do.

"I've lost them both."

CHAPTER TWENTY-THREE

"Aunt Romy?"

Romy's eyes widened a little as the girls sat beside her in the pew, Vienna on her left and Juliet on her right.

"Aunt Romy, are you okay?" Juliet asked.

"We didn't mean to scare you," Vienna said.

Romy looked at them and tried not to smile for fear that none of this was truly happening. "Is it really you?"

Vienna laughed softly. "Of course it is. We told you we'd meet you here at St. Anthony's right after your mass, remember?"

Romy took another minute to let it all sink in, and then tears of relief filled her eyes. She laughed.

"Oh, girls, I can't tell you how wonderful it feels to see you! To talk to you. I was having the strangest thoughts just now. Horrible, unspeakable thoughts." She held hands with them. "I'll tell you later."

"Maybe you'd better," Vienna said. "We're running a little late."

"For what?"

"We're meeting Mom and everyone else back at our house," Juliet said.

"Felicity?"

"We're all going out together," Juliet said. "Don't you remember?"

"We asked you to come with us," Vienna said, "but you said you had to bring paperwork home from the office and you'd be busy all weekend long."

Romy nodded. "So who's all going?"

"Mom, Victor, Maxi, Cassandra, and the two of us," Juliet said.

"All of you? Where are you going?"

"We don't know yet," Vienna said.

"Wow, all of you together," Romy said. "That's incredible. You must be looking forward to it."

Juliet smiled warmly. "We are."

"This has been a long time coming," Vienna said.

"You both seem so relaxed," Romy said. "So at peace. I'm very happy for you. That's all I ever wanted for you girls."

"We know that, Aunt Romy."

"So everything's okay," Romy said with a nod. "Everything's going to be okay."

"Of course it is," Vienna said.

"Do you girls know how much I love you?"

"Sure, we do," Juliet said. "We love you, too."

Vienna glanced at her watch. "I'm sorry, Aunt Romy, but we really have to go. Everyone is waiting for us."

Romy felt both joy and sadness when she heard those words, and they resonated in her mind over and over as she sat alone in the pew.

"Everyone is waiting for us."

www.ingramcontent.com/pod-product-compliance
Lightning Source LLC
Chambersburg PA
CBHW020342260626
47156CB00004B/1651